CHOWRINGHEE CHARMS

SUMITA BANERJEA

Readomania

Readomania
An imprint of Kurious Kind Media Private Limited
readomania.com
email: contact@readomania.com
Facebook: facebook.com/iamreadomania
Twitter: twitter.com/iamreadomania
Instagram: iamreadomania

First Published in 2021 by Readomania

ISBN: 978-93-91800-05-5

Typeset in Palatino Linotype by Shine Graphics
Printed in Delhi

Sumita Banerjea's style of writing reflects an ease with words and an elan that arises from the raconteur's confidence with the subject. Many of her stories transport the reader to the world of the upper middle class Bengali families and we get interesting and insightful glimpses into their world-views, their traditions, and the subtle nuances that distinguish their unique way of life.

—**Jawhar Sircar**, MP; former Secretary,
Govt. of India and ex-CEO, Prasar Bharati

Each story in this book has a different theme and cast of characters, but each creates drama and anticipation and builds up to a carefully-crafted resolution. Sumita Banerjea combines detailed and vivid descriptions that bring people and places alive with a frank but sensitive portrayal of the complex landscapes of human emotions and relationships.

—**Upinder Singh**, Professor of History
at Ashoka University and author

The twist at the end of the stories in this collection is what I enjoyed most. That surprise element makes them special.

—**Hima Kohli**, Judge,
Supreme Court of India

Readomania

India has traditionally been the land of storytellers and a lot of us have an inherent skill of creating good plots, good stories and good narrations. With a little encouragement and support, many more authors will be widely read and attain a place in the sun. This is the essence of *Readomania*—an initiative that nurtures emerging stars of the literary world.

It would not be an exaggeration to say that *Readomania* is the talent hunt in fiction. It goes a step beyond by not just identifying the talent but also nurturing it and showcasing it to the world. In the process, we have created a powerhouse of content.

Readomania has four principal interest areas—traditional print publishing, online library of short stories and poetry, literary events and products.

The print publishing works towards delivering good quality content to the readers. We publish good authors in meaningful anthologies, novels and works of narrative non-fiction. Our books stand out for their perspectives, the plots, the language and most importantly their ability to enrich lives.

Take a break, read something nice, write something beautiful. Read our books or visit us at www.readomania.com and enjoy a whole new world of literature.

Contents

Foreword 9

1. Chowringhee Charms 11
2. Brishti 26
3. Camouflage 38
4. Enmeshed 48
5. How About a Date? 57
6. Palash 70
7. The Mango Orchard 79
8. Unfinished 92
9. Refuge 102
10. Sadhan Chatterjee 109
11. Snake Family 122
12. Stopgap Hero 131
13. The Conch 140
14. The Foot Doctor 151
15. Wee-Wee Experiences 157
16. Aam Kheer 167
17. Why Not for Me, Ma? 175

About the Author 183

Foreword

A remarkable collection of short stories welcomes the reader to flights of imagination sailing smoothly from crime to the supernatural, angst of adolescence to marital discord. Woven in, occasionally, is a gentle query on values that sustain life.

This is Sumita Banerjea's first offering of short stories, though she is no stranger to writing. Her school textbooks on Geography and English have received wide acceptance and she has been a familiar contributor to magazines and journals. A teacher for many years, Banerjea's PhD thesis was on the distinctly macabre subject of 'Women Criminals of Bengal' in the 18th and 19th centuries and was followed by training in psychological counselling. Her own varied experience in interacting with history and people thus gives her creativity a rich patina of credibility where her characters step effortlessly on to the stage.

Young adults and their challenges occupy a noticeable share of the book. The author's empathy with her characters is palpable. Her pen starkly dissects the careless parents who have not cared to nurture the child but have only thrust their own ambitions and desires on their progeny, creating bitter burdens of expectations. Indifference to children in the pursuit of careers is not an uncommon phenomenon. Though the stories do not consciously reflect a feminist standpoint, accounts of existing realities dwell perforce on the uneven treatment meted to girls and women and their sterling ability to overcome the odds of parental discrimination and spousal indifference.

Banerjea's spirits do not frighten or intrude. They are usually gentle souls seeking fulfilment in union with their beloved or correcting some past wrongs. Prayers are offered to calm unrequited passions. And, on one occasion, a victim of murder does demand and obtain justice.

There are many more. Some touching on human frailties with amusement. Others dealing with sombre social issues. But what distinguishes Banerjea's work is her lightness of touch and her confidence in letting the reader draw their conclusions without the tedious crossing of the t's or dotting the i's. The crispness of plot and prose and the occasional twist in the tail reminds the reader of Bonophul and O'Henry.

Deb Mukharji
Former diplomat, photographer,
occasional author, and columnist

1

Chowringhee Charms

It all started with the visits to the auction house. As little children of nine, the twins, Kismet and Kahani, would wander around the musty, dusty, cobwebby lure of *Chowringhee Charms*, flicking the dust of history off the intriguing items on display. Enamelled door knobs, coloured glass figurines, incomplete bone China tea and dinner sets in the most delicate designs with rich gold dragons and floral fantasies, ancient watches and clocks in an array of shapes and sizes. Each visit was an escapade into an enchanted and magical long lost era, so different from and so much more absorbing than the clinical perfection of steel furniture and shiny tiles of their modern home. Each item had a story to tell and the twins would spend hours spinning tales around them and enacting them.

It was a Sunday morning treat they impatiently waited for and Mr Baltiwala would welcome them with his crinkly eyes and wide, toothless smile. In fact, he himself was a curiosity draw for the children. "So wha...at do I have for you this morn....ing, le...t me...eee see...," he would tease in his typical slow and tantalising style and the young visitors would wait with baited breath.

"He has finally found the missing twirl of the Chinese warrior's moustache," suggested Kismet, with hope shining bright on his excited face.

"I think he has located the secret key to the musical tea set," claimed Kahani, who true to her name was always imagining dramatic finales.

Mr Baltiwala had, in fact, found a wee key but it was for the entrance door to a replica of an ancient Scottish castle, of a size into which the children could enter. Stark and forlorn to look at, the castle had slits for windows, arched tall doors and even a steep winding staircase to a room on the first floor. It occupied a large part of the corner of the shop and since the building was very old with high ceilings, the double storied castle fitted in.

Mr Baltiwala explained that it was a remnant of the Raj. A senior British officer had imported it to amuse his wife and children and add a touch of home in a far off land. Once they left for their homeland a few years after India's independence, carrying the 'touch' seemed unnecessary. And, so, it had found its fate in the care of Mr Baltiwala who had procured it many years ago, for a princely sum of Rs 850. The twins were intrigued. The very thought of a historical home, within their own 21st century glass and tile room, was enough to get their little hearts pounding. Eagerly taking the key, they opened the creaking door and stepped into history. There was a little parlour with a mini hat and umbrella stand made of solid wood and a chest of drawers. Next to it was a small living room with chairs, a table, and a crockery stand. The stairs led into a bedroom with a bed, a chair, and a mirror on the wall.

Kahani, unable to resist the temptation, curled up in the small bed. She imagined herself as the princess in the castle with maids in waiting, pandering to her every wish. Their parents had read stories to them of kings and knights and they had also watched animated movies of life in the bygone era. In their summer holidays they had visited Edinburgh and taken tours of the grand castles. Their father was a well-known feature writer for newspapers and he often wrote travelogues as well while their mother worked for a publishing house of school textbooks.

A castle of one's own was a living fantasy. "I also want to lie on the bed," said Kismet who, though the same age, was indulgent towards his twin. "Get up and let me feel like a prince at least if not a king," he added.

"We'll take turns lying on it," suggested Kahani.

"Oh, you are talking as if we own it. We have to come to the shop every Sunday then," said Kismet.

"And, what if someone else buys it?" said the sage Kahani. This put the twins in a sombre mood. True. How could they experience the thrill of a royal life if the castle was not there?

"Do you think this could be our joint birthday gift?" suggested Kismet, with a hint of trepidation and hope.

"We have to be very good. Only then will Baba and Ma consider this idea," said Kahani. And, so they chitchatted as they played out their flights of fancy.

They could hear Mr Baltiwala pottering around outside, entertaining other customers when Kahani suddenly clutched on to Kismet's hand. She held on to his wrist with all her miniature might and whispered, "Did you hear that?" Looking at her ashen visage he instinctively held on to his sister, giving her comfort and support. Becoming completely silent, both strained their little ears to listen. It was definitely there, the sound of someone breathing, rather heavily, and it was very close to them. But they couldn't see anything or anyone. Their bodies stiffened as they held on to each other, terrified and also intensely curious. "Who or what do you think it is?" whispered Kismet. "Let's ask," braved the more daring Kahani. "Don't you think we should quietly go out and forget that this happened and not tell anyone? What if we get trapped here?" ventured Kismet. "And never know the answer to our question! Of course, not. I definitely want to know what this is all about," concluded Kahani with a determined tone, putting a firm stop to all speculation.

Knowing that she had her brother with her, Kahani mustered up all the courage she could and asked, "Who are you? What do you want?" A hundred other questions were storming through her head but she controlled herself. Did the 'sound' not understand English? Should the language have been Hindi or Bengali? Well, the 'breath' better understand her, Kahani thought to herself and waited, impatiently. No progress. What could they do? Just as she was reframing the questions in Hindi, Kismet pointed to the mirror with trembling fingers. Through a cloudy, smoky haze appeared a pair of eyes, surprisingly sharp and alert. It gradually focused on the twins. Their fingers clung and an otherwise brave Kahani was struck speechless. Gradually, through a parched mouth and hushed tone, she ventured, "Who are you? Is there something you wish to say?" While the eyes held them spellbound, the twins felt a warm breath brush their necks.

"W....what is happening?" quivered Kismet, "the eyes are somewhere and the breath is somewhere else. What do you want from us? You are scaring us." There, he had said it!

"Don't worry. I will not harm you. For years I have not been able to leave this room. Will you help me?" It was a woman. She spoke in English and her tone was not threatening. If anything, it was sad and helpless.

Feeling a little calmer, Kismet asked more confidently, "We are children. How do we help you? And who are you anyway? Why have you stayed trapped in this room and for how long?" The questions simply poured out like the proverbial water of India.

"So many questions! Which one should I answer first? I'll begin by introducing myself. My name is Maya and I was a governess to the children whose castle this was. Their mother stayed unwell most of the time. Blasted Calcutta weather, is what the master put it down to. You want to know how you can help? You see, I don't trust adults. They play games. Dirty ones. You can help me because you are children and you have pure hearts."

This was sounding more and more complicated. So, what did their 'pure heart' have to do with solving governess Maya's problems? Kahani had a more basic question. "So, as a governess, what did you do? Actually, I find it very difficult talking to air or a breath. Will you not show yourself?"

There was tinkling laughter and then Maya answered, "I don't know how to. I only know how to project the image of my eyes on the mirror, like a reflection. You just have to believe what I am saying. Look, there is not much time. You will soon need to go. If you look carefully, you will find a small latch under the bed. Lift it and you will see that the frame slides. Inside, there is a hollow that has some papers. Please take them out."

Her curiosity suitably roused, Kahani did as she was asked and found a sheaf of papers, yellowed and frayed. Acutely conscious that this was very important for voice Maya, she took it carefully, placed it on the bed, and asked, "What is this and why have you asked me to take it out?"

Kismet, eager to add his questions piped up, "Are they secret documents?"

"Well, you could say that they are," answered breath Maya. "If you look carefully, you will see that they are a collection of stories written by me. I loved writing and to entertain the children I created a series of stories around the characters based on those children. I gave them Indian names, *Aasman* and *Kiran* (sky and sunbeam). Both of them loved the outdoors and they were fascinated with the sky and clouds and birds and I made up tales of them jumping from cloud to cloud as their playground and raindrops as water fountains, little birds singing them lullabies, and white water crystal flowers reflecting the shades of sunlight..." The twins could sense that Maya was lost in her reverie, recounting happiness. What was strange was that a lot of what she was saying sounded very familiar.

"Oh, I wish someone would create custom made stories for us," exclaimed Kismet, excitement evident in his voice.

"Oh, do be quiet. You and your crazy wishes," chided Kahani and continued, "But what do the stories have to do with us, Maya?"

"So, this is where I need your help. You see...," there was a pregnant, palpable pause as the twins looked at the direction the voice appeared to be coming from. It was uncanny to talk to nothingness that appeared to be stifling tears but the situation demanded extra sensitivity and quiet respect. Maya seemed to have got her emotions under check as she continued, "I have been waiting all these years for a wrong, a criminal wrong, to be righted. That man, the master, stole my mind matter."

"What does that even mean?" the twins asked in unison.

"Well, he thieved the ideas conceived, created, and nourished in my brain. How would you like it if you spent hours of your energy, eagerness, word engineering, and mind crafting to create something beautiful and then someone simply robbed it? And, to top it all, he claimed that it was *his* work and *his* writing. Can you even imagine that? He simply gave my characters English names and published my mind under his name and became a celebrity. I feel cheated, violated, and extremely angry!"

"So, how can we right this wrong now? We would be mad if someone took away our craft work and claimed to have made it but we would have to prove it. How do we prove your story?" asked Kismet.

There was no hesitation with the answer. "As I said, I have faith in the goodness in children. My little wards loved my stories and this man made a big name and huge money out of them. He called the characters Welkin (sky or vault of the sky) and Sunshine; a rough translation of the names that I had given. The stories that I have given you were never seen by the man, otherwise he would have taken them too. So, they are the proof that I wrote the series. The style, ideas, and the spirit of the stories are the same. It is very clear that the creator is the same person. I have even illustrated some of the stories. Details about the family, where they stayed, and some pictures are also there with these papers. There are photographs of the four of them and me. The handwriting is mine and my signature is there at the end of the stories. He had taken the manuscript for the other stories, promising to get them published since he knew publishers in London, and I like a fool had trusted him. Please, do whatever you can and tell the world my story." And entrusting the twins with this enormous responsibility, voice Maya faded away in eye and sound.

Kismet and Kahani were in a quandary. What were they to do? No wonder they had found Maya's recollections of the tales familiar. Welkin and Sunshine were their favourite characters and they had read all the books in the series. The setting, their adventures in Skyland, their cloud school, and everything that happened there; they knew it all by heart. Both of them believed Maya and intuitively knew that justice had to be given to her so that she could rest in peace. And they understood all too well that it had to be them doing the needful. They had to be worthy of the trust reposed in them.

Clutching the precious papers carefully, they stepped out of the castle. Mr Baltiwala was busy with other people and Kismet went quietly to him and returned the key to the castle. "See you both again next weekend," he said affectionately and carried on with his work. The twins needed to come up with a plan but they could not do it alone. Who would believe them? Their experience would appear to be a figment of overactive imagination triggered by a toy castle of yesteryears. But that could not be an impediment to the goal they had set out to achieve.

A little later their parents found a surprisingly silent brother and sister waiting at the door of the shop. That was most unusual since the norm was that they had to be cajoled out of the auction house, most often with a promise of bubble gum ice-cream. Ma noticed the papers Kahani was protectively holding close to her chest. "What are those papers?' she asked. "Important documents," was the evasive reply from Kismet. Intrigued with what was going on, Ma and Baba wanted to investigate the papers once they got back home. Soon the twins blurted out the story that had been choking them and felt very relieved having shared their unique experience.

Initially, fairly disturbed with what they had heard, Ma and Baba gradually settled themselves and sat with the twins and went over the incident once again in detail. They then looked at the stories and the pictures. They knew their progeny well and recognised that this was no fantasy tale. They had obviously gone through a strange experience, inexplicable by logic. This was the area of the unknown, the misty firmament where the light glowed but not strongly enough to get a clear view. The existence of the light could not be denied, however weak its radiance. Even in the shadows, the cry of the wronged spirit pierced through unseen shrouds. The question now was, what next?

"We can't let her down. There must be something we can do to get her justice," exclaimed a visibly upset Kismet.

"It is her eyes we saw in the mirror. I can recognise them from the photograph, even though it is a bit faded. She had kind eyes," added Kahani, nearly in tears.

The parents could understand the agony and the helplessness of the children. The children needed to feel secure that their parents believed them and would do whatever was possible to help them fulfil their commitment to a troubled soul. "Okay, give us a couple of days and let us think over the matter. It is a tricky situation. No one will believe your story, so we cannot prove anything in court but we have the unpublished manuscript and that can certainly be put into a book. She also has some very fine illustrations that can go along with the stories," assured Ma.

"I will do some research regarding the details that are there about the family, where they lived, and Maya. Some archive might have records. Let us see," promised Baba. And so, the family went to bed that night, a little tense, a little restless but also hopeful.

In the weeks that followed, there was intense activity. Ma keyed in the stories into the computer and the original manuscript was scanned and saved for future use while Baba visited libraries and government archives to verify the details about the officer and his family. The officer's house had been a big mansion in the Fort William area and he had the reputation of having a sharp tongue and a volatile temper. His wife, a timid lady, lived a very restricted life under his hawk-like watch. The children were under the tutelage of an Indian woman, zesty Maya, who had been educated in a convent and had a mind of her own. For reasons unknown, the master did not meddle with her. Perhaps, he was a little bit in awe of her. Who knows, it might even have been stronger emotions that he harboured for her which were not reciprocated. Used to owning and getting what he desired, perhaps it was his diabolical way, by stamping his name on her creations, that he got to own a part of her that she was most proud of. She was coveted by other English families to look after their children but Maya was very attached to her wards and the promise of higher wages could not lure her away from them.

The officer had become famous as an author on his return to Britain from India and had died several years ago and so had his wife. There were no records of him having written anything else other than the stories of Welkin and Sunshine. It all seemed to fit in. He obviously was no natural storyteller.

Finally, after much consideration and thought, Baba conceived of a plan. He decided to write the story of Maya, as an ode to her enormous talent that had remained unsung. He spoke of her love for and faith in children, her tremendous ability to give the child mental wings and space, and a sense of liberation to explore unknown worlds, her facility with using the English language, the cruel trick that had been played on her, her determination to fiercely protect what she had given birth to and then proceeded to publish her hidden manuscript as a series, along with her photograph and her illustrations. No name was mentioned of the wrongdoer but every week, for the next few months, in a column entitled, 'The Sky Unbound', the adventures of Aasman, Kiran, and their ethereal friends were published.

As expected, children and adults responded spontaneously to the imagination, simplicity, and the uplifting quality of the stories. On popular demand, the stories were finally published into a beautiful book with Maya as the author and the cover was designed by Kismet and Kahani. They had not let breath Maya down. "Governess Maya, wherever you are, we hope you are at peace now. It was your belief in us that made it possible and our parents' faith in what we told them. We even put in our craft along with your mind matter. So, it is a kind of joint effort. Isn't that nice? There is a book release that has been planned and perhaps you would like to attend it," declared Kahani to the world at large as Kismet stood smiling next to her. Later, the twins firmly believed that they had felt a gentle breeze cocoon them, in the enclosed area, where the book release was held.

In another continent, Maya's wards, the children for whom the stories had been created, octogenarians now, also heard about the popularity of the new book through their great-grandchildren. With the reach of technology, the book had crossed many oceans. And they smiled. The innocent, pure, happy smile of a child that Maya had loved so much. Happy and relieved that Maya had finally got her due. Aware that the stories about Welkin and Sunshine had not been written by their father, the two children had always felt very ashamed and guilty, but terrified as they were of the man, they could not protest when he published them in his own name.

It is said that things have a way of going around and so it happened with the British siblings too. The call of their childhood and their curiosity to meet the persons who had discovered Maya's writings brought them on a visit to Kolkata. The twins and their parents too, were very eager to spend some time with them and invited them home to talk about their stay in India and learn more about the enigmatic Maya. Sitting in the drawing room, sipping tea, they exchanged notes. The octogenarian siblings were told the curious story behind the discovery of the hidden manuscript and in turn they reminisced about Maya. "She was more of a surrogate mother to us and taught us firm values, awakened in us the wonder of imagination, and put us on a magic carpet to fly and discover unknown realms. She would occasionally even cook exotic Indian dishes, creating a home for us in this wonderful land," recalled 'Aasman', nostalgically. As they slipped into the comfort of childhood, enthusiastically cradling the new book, ironically written for them decades ago, 'Kiran' made a request, "We are very eager to visit and experience the wonder of *Chowringhee Charms*. Do you think you could take us there, please?"

It was an entourage of six people who trouped in and Mr Baltiwala warmly welcomed them. When informed that the castle had originally belonged to the foreign visitors, he was astounded and amazed by the sequence of events. "Oh! That is quite astonishing. Who would ever believe that the owners of the castle are visiting my shop! I only have the inanimate mute objects of the past that cannot speak their tales. I would love to listen to your stories about this unique castle."

He was not privy to the information about the hidden documents. That remained a secret amongst the six members of Team Maya and they had pledged to keep it that way. What did follow appeared to be the most natural course of things. The siblings from overseas were emotionally overwhelmed on seeing the castle of their babyhood and decided to have it transported back to their country, as a special gift for their great-grandchildren and were more than willing to pay good money for it. Mr Baltiwala was overjoyed to get a windfall in pounds. The twins, though struck with a twinge of disappointment at first, at not being able to play Prince and Princess in their castle, understood the value it had for Aasman and Kiran and also realised the impossibility of keeping a castle in their modern flat.

"I am feeling a bit sad and happy at the same time. Does that sound odd?" asked Kismet with a philosophical expression.

"No, it doesn't. I feel the same way but we will soon grow too big to enter this castle and then what will we do with it? The castle has provided us an adventure of a lifetime and that will be our secret treasure," summed up the ever practical Kahani, lightly squeezing her brother's hands in a gesture of understanding.

What happened to voice Maya? She was released from her forced captivity of keeping vigilance over her mind property. Once it took life and wings into a book to reach children worldwide with her rightful name as the author, she felt emancipated, unburdened, and unshackled. With a light heart, full of gratitude that her deep conviction in goodness had been validated, she knew that she would meet her benefactors someplace else, at some other time, in some other lifetime. For now, she was free to soar and escape into her Skyland, where she could dance from cloud to cloud, raindrop to raindrop, carefree.

2

Brishti

Her parents named her Brishti[1]. Born alongside the first raindrop of the season as it bounced off the dusty earth, Brishti's arrival brought the scent of the parched soil soaking in life. Twenty-two years hence, she continued to radiate a fresh fragrance, now laced with the heady aroma of newfound love.

Bhalobasha[2] was in the air and she breathed it in, lustily. Tendrils of earthy passion unfurled within her, hesitantly. As he traced his finger, down the parting in her hair, colouring it red, during the marriage ceremony, she looked deep into her husband's eyes, startled by the intensity of her own emotions. She had known him only a short while and after the first few meetings, had completely trusted her heart into his keeping.

"Marriage suits you," her friends commented, after she returned from her honeymoon and she blushed happily, content with her man. Suave, courteous, good looking, passionate; what more could one ask for. Holidays over, she moved with him to a small town in Odisha where he had been posted for the past three years.

---

[1] Rain.

[2] Love.

An important official in the government, he had been allotted a sprawling bungalow, complete with a retinue of domestic help. The *chowkidar*[3] and *mali*[4] had been working for decades, but the cook and the driver were new recruits. The grounds of the house spread over several acres and Brishti would go off for a walk by herself, sometimes discovering a wild overgrown corner with big brown rabbits, that would stare at her with curiosity or an old unused well, in the dark and cool interiors of which she could hear the chatter of birds.

Life was laidback and undemanding and Brishti engaged herself with the garden and the house, adding that elusive woman's touch to a bachelor's abode. Occasionally she would cook a special dish that she knew her husband liked. "We will have dinner on the lawn this evening. The weather is just right for a bonfire. We could have some kebabs and parathas with your special phirni and we will round it off with the Baileys Irish Cream that you enjoy," suggested her husband before going to office. Brishti was thrilled with the idea.

Being an important man's wife in a small place, she was expected to participate in various welfare activities and interact with the local ladies. She made a few friends but had been told by her husband to maintain her distance, in keeping with her status. Life did get lonely sometimes but she brushed aside such feelings. After all, she had her husband to herself.

Over the months she had also gained confidence, and took an active role in some of the welfare projects

---

3 Watchman.

4 Gardener.

involving the tribal women like healthcare and microfinance schemes where the women took the lead in saving money for the family. Addiction to alcohol was an endemic problem and money in the hands of the man often meant that very little trickled into the hearth. It was a slow process to empower the women but Brishti hoped to make a difference with her encouragement and inputs. Her husband was not aware of her level of involvement, but there was a slow fire burning in Brishti to do something worthwhile.

She greeted her husband every evening, on his return from work, dressed in outfits that she knew he approved of and eagerly waited for the glint of appreciation in his eyes. Strong, earthy tones appealed to him. "Basic instincts, you see," he would say, laughing at himself.

After living an idyllic life for a little over a year, Brishti discovered that she was with child. Nothing could have made her happier. Gently patting her abdomen she spoke to the tiny life breathing inside her, assuring it of all her love and care. "I am waiting for you. You will make our lives complete. From now on, I will be especially careful about what I eat and my exercises so that you are healthy and strong. I can't wait to hold you in my arms."

One evening her husband informed her that he would be away on tour for a fortnight, visiting some of the remotest areas in the district. "Living conditions there are very basic even in the guest houses and travelling by car on the *kucchha*[5] roads will be very uncomfortable and perhaps dangerous for you. So, it is advisable for

---

[5] Unpaved.

you to stay home." Brishti would usually accompany him on his tours but this time she agreed with him, a little uncomfortable with the idea of staying alone in the huge house, but she put up a brave front. It was decided that the maid would sleep in for fourteen days.

The day of his departure dawned a mellow golden with the faint hint of light on the eastern sky. The sun was still waking up when he left. Drugged with sleep and love, she bade him farewell and stood a while until she could no longer see the jeep. It was chilly and she covered herself, taking care to keep warm. She had two people to look after now.

Sleep by then had forsaken her and she decided to bathe and get ready for the day. Her bedroom had a large four poster bed, an easy chair, and a dressing table next to which was a little ante room with white chintz curtains. As she sat in front of the mirror a shiver shot through her, almost like an electric shock. Was she seeing right? Reflected in the mirror was a pair of dark feet with heavy silver anklets under the transparent lace curtain. They were a woman's feet. She could see no form above that. Brishti swung around in a panic. The feet were gone.

Her body was flushed and hot and her mind in total disarray. Almost hysterical with fear, she walked around the house. There was no logical explanation and she was too wide-awake for it to have been anything but a real experience. She had no one to discuss it with in the house and was sure it would be 'poofed' off as wild imagination if she called her husband. She could almost hear him joke, "Just a couple of hours of being on your own and you've started seeing things! Think of something more creative to get me back quickly."

Somehow, the minutes stretched into hours. Sitting with a book in front, flipping pages, Brishti read nothing. The lace curtain had developed its own magnetic field and her eyes went there involuntarily. As the shadows lengthened, a dread fell upon her. That night as she sat in front of the mirror to comb her hair she saw the feet again, alive and vibrant, without a body on top. The woman appeared to be standing there, waiting and watching.

Who did the feet belong to? Why was she there? What did she want? Was she trying to tell Brishti something? Questions ravaged her mind and she ran out of the room, choked with terror.

The lights stayed on in the house that night and Brishti slept in another room, with the maid sleeping on a mattress on the floor. The sheer presence of another human near her gave her some support. She slept fitfully, convinced that the feet were following her, eager to attract her attention. They were visible only to her. This went on for the next few days till her nerves were stretched to snapping point.

Practically driven out of her mind, she spoke to the old *mali* with whom she had developed an affectionate relationship. "*Bahurani, kya baat hai? Aapki tabiyat to theek hai*?[6]" he asked. Not knowing how to bring up the topic, she asked him if there was any tribal girl who had stayed in the house earlier. The old wrinkled face lost colour

---

[6] Madam, is something the matter? Are you feeling all right?

and he looked very alarmed. *"Kyon, kuch hua kya?*[7]*"* he asked, his voice hoarse and scared.

She knew then that there was a story that was being kept under wraps. With a lot of persuasion she finally discovered that before her marriage, a tribal girl, Bindiya, was working as a cook in the house and she stayed in the quarters provided for the servants. She was an attractive young woman who was unmarried but came to be with child and was thrown out by her family. *"Phir kya hua? Ab woh kahan hai?*[8]*"* she asked. The old man looked away with a sad and forlorn expression.

Brishti realised that to get to the bottom of the story she would need to do some investigation on her own. Not finding out was not an option. And help from the *mali* would be limited, though he did provide the directions to Bindiya's home. It was a determined Brishti that went to Bindiya's house, pretending to be a journalist, working on women's issues. Her village was far away and not in one of the areas which Brishti frequented to help the local women. This was fortunate because she was an unknown entity in that area and the family members were ready to talk.

There was a picture of a young, vivacious girl on the wall with dancing eyes and another one of the same girl with a puzzling, sad expression. The parents were angry but helpless. They told her that Bindiya had confronted the man who had made her pregnant and there had been a huge row. A spirited girl, Bindiya had decided to

---

[7] Why, has something happened?

[8] And what happened after that? Where is she now?

have the child against his wishes. She had informed her parents and they had not been in favour of her decision. She continued to work and soon after she died under mysterious circumstances. The parents were convinced that the man in question had killed her.

Being a man with enormous clout, the matter had been completely hushed up and it was reported as suicide by consuming poison. The cause of the suicide given was the shame she felt because of her pregnancy since she was not married and had been ostracised by her family. Bindiya's parents had been painted as the culprits for disowning her and pushing her to suicide. "*Driver to gawah tha par use rupyon se chup kara diya gaya. Ab woh doosri jagah kaam karta hai. Paison se zameen khareed kar ek ghar banaya hai. Vishwas nahin ho to aap uska gaon jakar pata kar sakte hain*[9]," she was told. A sick feeling came over Brishti and she asked for the name of the man.

It was her husband.

She realised then that Bindiya had come to her for assistance. She wanted justice. In Brishti, she hoped to find the understanding since both of them shared the same man. Bindiya had waited patiently, convinced that her story would be revealed to Brishti and now that she too was pregnant, she would empathise even deeper.

Overnight, the young and happy mother to-be, grew years older. Torn by conflicting emotions, she was in a quandary about her next course of action. Had her

---

[9] The driver was a witness but he had been silenced with money. He bought a piece of land with that money and has built a house. If you don't believe this, you can go to his village and check it out.

husband actually done such a thing? Could she believe the evidence she had gathered? All those blissful times spent with him, should she believe that image of him that she had experienced or the other one? Could she live with a cold-blooded murderer? Would Bindiya ever leave her in peace if she chose to overlook her husband's past? *Could* she ignore a past like this one? Her entire being was in turmoil as she struggled to find a direction.

Then, quite suddenly, a calm descended on her. Her tangled mind cleared up and she knew what she had to do. It was almost as if Bindiya and she got fused into one and she lived the intense agony of the murdered girl. She would not let him get away. Regardless of the happy times spent with him, there obviously was a cruel criminal residing in him who could be stoked under duress. She would never feel safe with him.

Two weeks later her husband came back from his tour, full of stories of all the good work he was doing for the tribals in the remote areas. "These tribals have been marginalised for so long. They have never got their rights. Their simplicity and trusting nature has been exploited all these years. It is time to give them their due."

"That is wonderful to know. What do you propose to do?" she asked.

"I have sanctioned some primary healthcare centres and schools. The women are very hardworking and we are trying to set up some self-help groups through which they can market the products they make," he replied enthusiastically, hoping to impress his wife and gain points with his superiors to ensure his promotion.

She played along with him for a while and then told him about the visit of a girl called Bindiya. "She said she knows you very well and will be coming again very soon. Bindiya says you are a kind man and will help her with her young son who she wants to put into a good school. She wants her son to be like you. I felt very proud of you. I didn't know that you have done so much social work."

His face turned ashen and he denied knowing anyone by that name. He asked Brishti not to encourage her. "Be careful of these women. You are gullible and they will take you for a ride." So, she let the matter rest for a couple of days.

She could sense that he was preoccupied and tense. After three days, she showed him things belonging to Bindiya (that Brishti had collected from her village home). "Bindiya had come again today and presented me with this silver necklace and bangles. She told me that you would never take anything from her but she feels very indebted to you for having helped her family. Such an attractive and sweet natured girl."

He got furious and for the first time Brishti saw terror in his eyes. "I told you not to encourage her. If this goes on I will have to send you back to your parents' home. She is not to be trusted."

Brishti had got her first cue. "Oh! But how do you know that she is untrustworthy? You said you don't know her."

"They are all the same, uncivilised, manipulative, and out to make a quick buck," came his reply.

"That is odd. Just the other day you said that their simplicity had been exploited," she answered.

Caught off guard, her husband was livid. "Look here. Are we going to argue about some strange woman who has been filling you in with all sorts of nonsense? In your condition, you need to rest and relax."

Brishti had summoned up courage to take on her husband. In a strange way, fighting for another woman's cause gave her added strength. Especially so in a situation where the wronged person could not personally fight for her cause, and was entirely dependent on Brishti.

She knew that she was at risk. He was a man who was always used to getting his way and things seemed to be getting out of his control. She had realised that she could not play the game all alone and needed an accomplice and took the old *mali* into confidence. He belonged to Bindiya's village and knew that she had visited her family and had learnt the truth. As matters got more tense, she asked him to stay inside the house at night, within calling distance.

One evening, after dinner, Brishti casually told her husband that Bindiya would be visiting them in a short while. "She is absolutely determined to meet you," she said.

This was the last straw. He got up from the chair and screamed at her, "I don't know what is going on. How can she meet me when she is not alive?" He was like a man possessed. There was fear, desperation, and anger steaming out of him.

Brishti continued, "But that cannot be. I have met her many times. Do you want me to believe that I am seeing and talking to a ghost?"

In a hysterical frenzy he shouted, "I don't know what you are seeing but she does not exist. She is dead. I know because I killed her." And then he realised what he had done.

In a fit of rage, he lunged at Brishti and put his hands around her throat. The tapering fingers whose caress had thrilled her, now dug deep into her veins. She struggled as his grip tightened and then she had a blurred image of there being many more people in the room in the next few moments. The *mali* had called the *chowkidar*, the cook, and the driver and together they held her husband and pinned him down. She called the local police officer and he was arrested for trying to strangle her. There were enough witnesses.

The trial went on for a long while. Bindiya's case was reopened and she finally got justice. Detailed investigations revealed the shop from where a lethal injection had been bought by the driver. During the second round of aggressive questioning, the driver broke down and confessed that he had bought it for his employer and had been paid handsomely for keeping quiet about it.

And Brishti? What did she get out of it? She could not bring herself to hate the man she had loved but she would not have been able to live with herself, protecting a murderer. In her quieter moments, when she was by herself, she wept tears of disappointment of her idyllic romance being shattered, of her dream family being broken.

And then, when her tears had washed away her unhappiness, she felt relief, almost like a deliverance from an evil grip after the freedom and liberation of Bindiya. Divorce was inevitable. Life had dealt her a strange hand. In her case, a set of strange feet. She remembered her last meeting with Bindiya. As she had turned around to have a last look at her bedroom before leaving the house forever, the ebony coloured, anklet-adorned feet, stepped out from behind the curtain and came close to her. Brishti was not afraid. She felt the carved heavy silver anklets being fastened around her ankles. The dark feet were bare. "Thank you, Bindiya," she whispered.

(This story was first published by the author in the Calcutta Club's magazine, *The Elite.*)

3

Camouflage

Relina was feeling gently toasted, warm, and crisp. The friendly winter sun spread its beams over the imposing edifice of St. Paul's Cathedral and lit up the historic stained glass windows. Sunlight poured into the church and those attending Sunday morning mass gazed in wonder at the paintings on the panes. It looked ethereal, as if a divinity had come riding on the slanted sunbeams and was being welcomed by the music of the church choir and organ.

She was sitting on the grounds of the National Museum, adjacent to the cathedral. Having been to church, she had strolled across to the classical monument. The images of the church had kindled her creative urge. She wanted to paint her memory of the rainbow of feelings that had moved her. Capture the lilting, soulful notes of the hymns in smoky shades of blue and green, illuminate the exuberance of the smiles exchanged, greetings in tones of yellow and orange, hold on to the powerful stillness and sanctity of the church in shades of the ocean depths. If only she could reproduce her painted memory on paper! Nothing else would give Relina a greater sense of attainment.

The steeples gleamed in the sunlight, the sky blushed, kissed by the tall spires. "Fertile imagination," Rathi would tease her as she romanticised about everything around her, painting love colours even onto inanimate objects. She understood the colour of love. Her strokes understood. Her palette did. "Everything can feel love. Even a doorknob is sensitive to the touch of affection or a rough push. Look at the door handles of old buildings. You can tell which ones have flourished with tender care and the ones that have withered. It is just that our wavelength is not tuned to their voices," she reasoned, passionately.

Rathi would join her in an hour and she wanted those moments of peace and solitude to consolidate her thoughts. A sketchpad was her constant companion and she quickly took it out, to put down her emotions in flowing strokes on to the paper. A student of the College of Fine Arts, the subject had been her passion for as long as she could remember. Relina was good at drawing portraits and now wished to draw portraits of emotions, and animate them through images.

The clock ticked away and an hour later she noticed that Rathi was still nowhere in sight. He was meant to join her at 9 am. It was now a little after 10 am. She tried calling him but his phone was switched off. She then decided to visit a small teashop close by. "Dada, could you make me a double egg fry with a lot of black pepper and cook it well on both sides please? I would also like two butter toasts along with a big earthen cup of your famous masala tea." It was a favourite meal and invariably lifted her spirits. She had not had breakfast and the morning's activities had made her hungry.

The historic museum stood solid and imposing in front of her, white, pristine, glorious, and grand. The stone walls had a look of wisdom and reliability, the ideal house for priceless treasures. The ribbed columns in front, the open arched façade along the long corridors that led into display rooms, the elegant teakwood staircase, conspired to exude majesty.

The museum had been shut to the public for renovation and she saw a few people moving about in the wide verandah running in front of the rooms, packing some items that seemed to have been taken out of the galleries. Relina was fascinated with art history and the museum drew her. More than once she had stolen away from her outings with her friends, to visit a new exhibition. Sometimes the exhibits were from the museum archive and the most recent was one on the Egyptian civilisation. It was a collaborative project with the Egyptian government and rare and priceless items had been brought in. Other than the mummies that had been a huge draw, Relina was mesmerised by the intricate jewellery, the papyrus paintings, and the exquisite pottery. Egyptian mythology and the philosophy of life after death had always intrigued her and the chance to see, touch, and feel history gave her goosebumps.

Once again, her eyes strayed to the watch, and she noticed that Rathi was late by well over an hour. So typical of him, she thought to herself. No point in fretting and fuming. She might as well do what she loved best.

So, out came her sketchbook once again. The sun had climbed and so had the temperature. She found herself a large, gnarled banyan tree and sat in its shade. The character of the magnificent building in front was an attractive subject and she busied herself drawing and framing it. The movement of the people working in the verandah, the trees standing guard, and the flight of stairs gave life to the silent structure.

She worked with concentration to ensure a proportionate replication of the building. And also the three dimensional feel, like a photograph. The still building was breathing, as palpably like the four young men and the woman whose movements and facial features were frozen in the sketch. Three of the men had beards, one of them also had long unruly hair. "I am so glad Rathi is not like his arty friends who believe that to be accepted in the club of artists and intellectuals they need to look unkempt," thought Relina to herself. Her man was clean shaven, lean, brushed his teeth to a sparkle, did not reek of stale cigarette smoke, and sported his full head of hair in a crew cut.

Rathi arrived well over two hours late, looking sheepish, and apologised profusely. "I was in Chandankot. The ferry service had some problem today and we were all stranded." Clad in a loose-flowing kurta and churidars, he looked as handsome as ever. She felt her anger melt away. He had that effect on her, ever since she had first seen him in college, a little less than a year ago, standing next to the tea shop, cheeks sucked in on a deep puff of a cigarette, a habit he had subsequently quit. His childlike pranks, easy manner, and interest in a wide variety of books had captured her heart. She knew that he was adept at spinning yarns and it was difficult to tell truth from fiction. Then, why did she put up with him? Stupid question she answered herself. She loved him. Blindly. He would crinkle up his languid eyes, smile the charming smile, follow it up with an easy joke, and she would be lost. She couldn't match his words or his charm. Putty. That was what she was. Humble clay in his hands, to mould as he wished. And he knew innumerable little ways to make her feel special. Like making a short film on her, surprising her with little love notes he would leave for her in her book, her shoes or her handbag, cooking a meal of her favourite dishes....

"What were you doing in Chandankot?" she asked, quite bewildered by this sudden visit. "I was taking a look at the promenade and meeting a group of young boys who are masters at doing any lighting work. I am planning a documentary on them and their amazing skill of creating magic with lights. Let those in Times Square come and see what our rural boys can do with practically no resources. All the major events in the city that need lights on specific themes use their services. They are also well up on the latest international developments which they portray through their lighting designs."

Relina felt her heart fill with pride. Here was her Rathi, the eternal dreamer, a student of film studies who hoped he would bring about his own revolution through the medium of cinema. "Are you hungry? I have gorged on butter-toast and eggs. Have something before we go anywhere else," she said.

"Actually I am starving. Hadn't realised it till you mentioned food. It has been a busy morning. Let us go to the café nearby. Coffee would be a great start."

Relina shut her sketchbook and together they went for coffee, followed by their planned outing to the Botanical Gardens. It was a bit of a hike but they had the entire day to enjoy the sprawling garden with its landmark great banyan tree, known to be one of the largest trees in the world, the orchids, the lakes with the giant water lilies, and all the other rare plants and trees.

The next morning, Relina woke contented and at peace. Yesterday had been a beautiful day with Rathi. They had walked around the park, had lunch at a small roadside *dhaba,* and spent the evening in Rathi's house, exploring each other in multiple ways. "I feel so comfortable with you. You are truly my soulmate. We enjoy doing the same things and spending time with you calms me and energises me. I had been tense this morning wondering whether the documentary would be possible, whether the deal with the foreign financiers would go through but being with you eased away all the tension. I need you to support me all the time," said Rathi, as the evening drew to a close. Relina just held him tight in response, assuring him of her love and commitment.

She had that languid morning-after feeling. She made herself a cup of fresh, aromatic tea, stretched herself on the couch, and browsed the newspaper.

Her eyes caught the headline, "Priceless Egyptian antiques stolen from the museum in broad daylight". Relina shot up, mortified. Reading on, she discovered the theft had occurred when she was sitting on the lawn, drawing her sketch of the museum. What a coincidence! After the initial shock, she felt enraged. How dare anyone do this? It bothered her. She carried the feeling with her until lunch, when a family friend was visiting her and they were to have lunch together. He was with the police, and she hoped to get more details from him about the theft.

As soon as Uncle Ravi arrived, Relina brought up the subject. "I read about the theft in the museum. It is appalling. I had been to the exhibition. It must have been done by those who knew the internal system. Strangely, through sheer coincidence, I was sitting in front of the building and sketching the scene, around the time the theft happened. There were some people moving around some boxes."

An astute policeman, Uncle Ravi asked to see the sketch. "It was carried out by a gang who specialise in art theft. It is obviously very big money and there is an international link. Replicas had been made of the items that were stolen and put in place of the originals. This was noticed by one of the employees of the museum who specialises in Egyptian art. He observed that one of the items in the cupboard did not look right and on further scrutiny found others that were copies too. It was done yesterday when the gallery was being cleaned and the artefacts were being put back after the renovation work was over. We are looking at all the leads possible to crack this and perhaps your sketches will help."

Relina happily took it out and showed it to him. He appeared to be interested in the men captured vividly in the sketch and asked if he could get it checked by the detectives to get facial matches. "Oh, I would be delighted if my drawings can help in bringing the criminals to justice," replied an enthusiastic Relina.

A couple of days later, Uncle Ravi called her to his office. She saw her sketch on the desk in front of him and an artist's impression of a closer view of the men, minus the beards three of them wore, and what appeared to be wigs. The features were now clearly visible without the camouflage. Computer simulations had been made and she saw the enlarged version on the screen.

Relina felt the world whizzing around her. Her throat felt constricted and her legs appeared to give way. She quivered as she stood in shock and disbelief.

There in front of her was the image of her very own Rathi!

Ravi, on seeing her, realised that something was very wrong. "Do you recognise someone, Relina? Look carefully to be sure. Your sketches have been of remarkable help. Two of these boys have been on our radar but we had no proof. They are a part of an international racket and are wanted in three cases."

Torn between her loyalty to Rathi and the realisation that he was a criminal who needed to be brought to justice, Relina was in agony. Being associated with the art world, he had gained access to the museum as a member of the renovation team. She understood the importance of her role in apprehending the gang. "Yes," she replied, softly. "I do recognise one of them."

"Can you tell us his whereabouts and phone number so that we can call him right now to ask him where he was on Sunday morning?" requested Ravi.

Shortly afterwards, a call was put through to Rathi, but not before a team of policemen had been sent to his home to nab him in the event he tried to make an escape. It was a relaxed and suave voice that took the call. "Hello," said Ravi, "Am I speaking to Mr Rathi?"

"Yes, you are. Where are you calling from?"

As the conversation progressed, Rathi was informed that the police wanted to know his whereabouts on Sunday morning.

"I was with my girlfriend from early in the morning and we spent the entire day together. You could check with her. She will vouch for me. What is this all about?"

Ravi wanted the phone number to contact her which Rathi said he would message. He did, but not before making a call to Relina.

When the phone rang, Relina took a moment to compose herself and picked up the telephone, after putting it on speaker so that the police could record it.

"Hello," she said.

"Darling, listen to me carefully. You will get a call from the police and they will want to know if I was with you from early in the morning on Sunday. Please tell them I was. I will explain things to you later. Do this for my sake, for our love's sake. Trust me. I will talk to you later." Saying this he cut the line, sure that he would not be investigated since his alibi was foolproof.

But it was not. Relina, the artist trumped Relina, the girlfriend, after a war within was won by the former.

The police arrested Rathi when he predictably headed for a safehouse, shortly after speaking to Relina.

4

Enmeshed

Her plait was her pride and her bane. Spanning all her five feet two inches, it walked behind her, supine in form, regal in bearing, rich and lustrous in texture. It had carved its own identity, separate from that of Badalini, from whose crest it hung.

Badalini[1] had been given her name because of her black mane that seemed to billow around her head like dark thunder clouds, ever since she was a babe. So, interestingly, it could be said that her tresses had given her a distinct identity. The hair and the person were almost like siblings, squabbling for attention. Stretching it further, they were like Siamese twins, joined by birth, yet two individuals fighting for their place under the sun. The trouble was that Badalini loved the attention that her hair commanded from everyone around her, and at the same time it overshadowed *her*—the person inside her slight frame.

Her hair had a will of its own. She remembered the oily hours when the whole world smelt of coconut oil, as her mother fed fistfuls of it to her greedy locks. The curls would defy any attempt to straighten them,

---

[1] Cloud.

and Badalini felt frustration mounting as the wiggles sprung from the tight braid and followed their wayward path.

"Ma, I am just tired of the time it takes to wash, clean, oil, and tie my hair. I get fed up. My friends with short hair can get it styled, blow dried, and they look so stylish and fashionable. I am stuck with a boring braid."

"My child, don't get so impatient. Have you forgotten our *samskaras*[2]? Do you not know the high pedestal on which hair has been placed in our culture? In our *shastras*[3], I was told, it is forbidden to catch hold of someone by the hair or drag a person by the hair, even in a fight. It is an act of dishonouring the person and the punishment could be severe and harsh. I have also heard that in some cultures, long hair is supposed to give one a sixth sense, like an extension of our nervous system. It acts like an antenna!

Think of all our goddesses, Lakshmi, Saraswati, Durga. How beautiful they look with their long, black locks! Which woman will not desire their qualities and their looks? They are the embodiment of beauty in every way, *stree shakti*[4], knowledge, and the arts. Aim to be like them, inside and outside. Those without naturally beautiful hair, resort to all kinds of artificial styling. It is the flaunting of the *kritrim*[5] and the superficial, today. You are beautiful the way you are.

---

[2] Hindu rites and rituals.

[3] Ancient Hindu texts.

[4] Female power.

[5] Artificial.

Even our lifegiving river, Ganges, is said to have been trapped in the locks of Lord Shiva, from where she was released eventually. Imagine the power of the *jatas*[6] of our *Jatadhara*[7]. The mighty river did not flow out of his palms or his mouth. So, never underestimate the importance of your treasure," explained her mother, giving her an insight into her cultural heritage.

Young Badalini was not convinced, petulant as she was, being unable to experiment with being trendy. Who was interested in gods and goddesses and their virtues, when real life with all its pleasures, was skipping her by?

But, somewhere, the message had got stored, to be accessed when required.

There were times when she loved her hair too. She remembered the occasion when her favourite drama teacher, Miss de Mellow, called her aside and asked, "Badalini, darling, would you like to play the part of Rapunzel in our annual school play? We can use your long braid very effectively! I have written the script in rhyme and we were planning on a musical production this year. The music teacher has written the score for the music, based on the script."

Badalini was beside herself with joy. The opportunity to play the lead role, all because of her natural attribute, called for a truce with her hair. Besides, the play being a musical, she was required to sing her lines. She put in hours of practice, to ensure her live singing performance

---

[6] Locks.

[7] Lord Shiva, who is said to have had a head full of matted hair.

was perfect. Hadn't her mother said that the goddesses were the role models? In this case, she prayed to Saraswati, the goddess of learning and the arts, to help her. Needless to say, the combination of her labour and her natural attribute, ensured a performance that won her a standing ovation.

But not everyone shared her joy. Her popularity and achievements meant that it was difficult to find fault with her or pity her in any way.

"Shorten the length," her distant aunt told Badalini's mother, in her presence. "The black rope will devour all the food that you feed your daughter. See how thin she is and how fat and healthy the parasitic twine is. This has become an obsession with you. It has become your trophy, but have you thought how difficult it is for the poor girl? Look at my daughter Rani. She has very healthy hair, but it does not rob her of her complexion. Everyone comments on her colour and her skin."

These words cut deep into Badalini's psyche. She was young and suggestive to comments around her. A fair complexion was held as the benchmark for beauty and she did not match up. "My hair is not allowing me to look as fair and pretty as Rani," she complained to her mother.

"Hush," her mother replied, "it is your treasure. Ma Kali is much darker, but is she not beautiful? Be happy with what you have. These people are jealous. When you grow up, you'll get many eager suitors lining up because of your beautiful locks. Just you wait.

Besides, remember how blessed you are. If ever you need a special wish fulfilled, you can always offer your hair as a sign of gratitude when your prayers are answered. How many women can make such a magnificent offering? It is a symbolic gesture of surrendering your ego and your vanity to the Almighty. And, even after your offering, your hair will grow back."

And so, Badalini had to be pacified and content with the hope that one day her locks would be her fortune and bring her fulfilment. The oiling sessions were followed by the washing ritual and her mother took enormous pride in untangling the mane as it unfurled from the towel and cascaded on to the paper that had been kept on the ground. Badalini would sit in the sun and dry her tresses.

And, as the little girl filled out into womanhood, her hair straightened a bit and her mother would put perfumed smoke through it. Her classmates stared at her braid in envy and passed caustic comments about it, equating it to a witch's wand.

Badalini, by then, had grown accustomed to this attention and the hurtful remarks. In the past twenty-two years, her hair and she had shared a tumultuous relationship, and had now reached a stage of peaceful co-existence. She still felt pangs of regret that people often overlooked her own skills and, most importantly, her well-endowed grey matter, and were mesmerised by her hair instead. It was like a self-created competition!

That is, until Amrit entered her life. Her first interaction with him was thanks to her dangling plait. As she got up from her seat to get off the bus, her head felt a tug, and she turned around to see that the pleasant-looking young man next to her seat was sitting on her braid. Apologising profusely, he released her hair and she smiled at his embarrassed confusion.

There was an instant spark in their chemistry. They often travelled in the same bus, by conscious choice, since they had got to know each other's timings. And, so began their courtship, which culminated in marriage.

Badalini took care to perfume her hair with a light floral fragrance that Amrit loved and he would bury his face in her silken locks as she clung to him. Both students of science, doing research in physics, they would feed off each other's minds and bodies.

"You turn me on in more ways than one," he bantered, as they got into a furious argument over a complicated problem in physics. He was trying to distract her as she got all charged up. And then, as they made up in bed, he would run his fingers over her back through the velvet strands.

"Do you know that you have one white hair that stands out conspicuously?" he asked her one evening.

"Yes," she replied. "I've been told that it is a sign of my mother's blessing. My hair is actually her doing. It is she who took care of it and taught me to value it. Left to myself, and under the influence of those around me, I probably would have 'scissored' it long ago. I have had this love-hate relationship with my hair."

"No, never cut it. Remember, it is your hair that brought us together. I have a right over it too!"

So, Badalini and her hair gradually became friends, having graduated from just co-existing to learning to be comfortable with each other and enjoying each other.

It was a public holiday, and Amrit and Badalini decided to go for a movie. The theatre had the modern, comfortable, sliding seats. Armed with nachos and coffee, they lost themselves in the film. Emotionally driven, the movie kept the hall engrossed, and even after it was over it took the audience longer to get off their seats and walk out.

Discussing the story, the two stepped into a café for a bite, and as Badalini turned to take her seat, Amrit called out to her sharply. "When did you cut your hair?"

"What are you talking about?" she asked, alarmed, and put her hand up to discover that her braid was missing below her waist. She couldn't believe what her hands were telling her. Checking frantically once again, she realised this was no bad dream. It was a harsh reality, and a shocking one. Somebody had snipped her hair in the movie hall and stolen her braid.

Badalini was devastated for days. No amount of consoling that it would grow back soon could help her. All her bitter-sweet memories with her hair ran through her mind as she mourned the loss of her twin.

And there were those who were only too willing to fuel her pain with fear. "This is a bad omen. Someone with dark energy is trying to bring you harm. They use personal belongings like clothes, hair or nails to influence evil powers against you. Through these items they gain direct access to you to victimise you. It comes from greed, fear or envy. Perhaps, the person is jealous of your happy marriage or your success at work. You must take the necessary help from those who are good with knowledge of paranormal activity, to neutralise these negative influences. Look at you. You appear to have the symptoms of being in the grip of black magic."

Badalini was a student of science. Though this talk did cause her uneasiness momentarily, her logical brain talked her out of its negative clutches. Also, her mother's words, that if she had done no wrong, she would be protected from all harm, by her faith in the Supreme Power, came to her rescue.

Slowly, she limped back to her regular life. One evening, walking down the footpath along a bustling Kolkata road, window-shopping, her eyes were drawn to a long braid hanging in the showcase of a beautician's shop. She looked carefully and felt her pulse racing. Running down the braid was one white hair.

She rushed in and asked if the plait was for sale. Bewildered by the request, the owner took the braid from the case and Badalini held it tenderly. "You see, it is mine," she said, tears glistening in her eyes. "I was lost without my friend. Can I have her back, please? I will buy her from you."

The shop owner realised that a unique and emotional moment was unfolding before him, and gifted the braid to her. He could sense the depth of her feeling, and understood that the hair would mean much more to her than it would to him.

Badalini went home, a happy and contented woman with a song in her heart. She pinned the braid to her hair and felt complete. Her hair would grow. But until such time, she had brought home her other half. Who knows, some day she would even offer her hair as an offering of gratitude!

5

How About a Date?

"It's been six months now since you have been staying apart. We had decided that you would take a call on how to proceed, after this period is over. So have you both made up your minds?" asked the marriage counsellor, Mrs Singh. The couple looked at each other, and having discussed the matter, informed her that they would like to give the marriage another shot.

"Is there any common thread that gave you this realisation? Could you tell me the happiest memories of your time together?"

"The initial years," came the spontaneous, joint response from both of them.

Mrs Singh smiled at the immediate reply. "Good. We have a platform from where we can start the next phase of your journey together. One option could be to go on a date and meet each other as strangers. And actually live the role, trying to discover each other anew. The other would be to pick up from where you left and see how it goes, now that you have the benefit of a different perspective, having lived apart for a while. Talk it over and take a call. We will meet again after fifteen days. There are a few communication techniques that we have to keep in mind, remember?"

They were both aware of it. The sessions with Mrs Singh had ensured that. Speak in 'I' sentences, stating your feelings, without blaming; speak respectfully and not belittle each other in any way, and most importantly, listen to the other person without formulating a response in the mind while the person is speaking. "Often it is the unsaid that is most crucial. You can understand that if you look at where the person is coming from, the 'feeling well' inside which the source is hidden and is often unexpressed. You are not at war, you are communicating to understand each other," she had explained. Easier said than done, but they were willing to give it a try.

Rupsa powdered her fifty-four-year-old nose. Small and sharp, the light catching the sparkling facets of the tiny diamond, it had a character. It meant business and spelt efficiency, and in the shadow play of light and darkness, it exuded femininity and softness.

Deep inside her she felt stirrings of a primordial passion, an excitement that refused to be curbed. It fluttered around her abdomen, in her chest, and her throat, rising up to flush her cheeks.

Rupsa gave a quick look around to see if anyone had noticed the beat of her quickening pulse and the slight breathlessness that went with it.

Thankfully, no. There was no one else in the privacy of the cloakroom in her office. She had taken half the day off from work. She stood in front of the full-length mirror, and adjusted the maroon and mustard pleats of her handloom sari, stepping on the border with little jerks to adjust the length around her heels.

A dash of kohl, a pat of brown lip lustre, and a light brush to get the bounce in her styled, shoulder-length hair, all adding up to her 'carefully casual' appeal, and she was ready. Ready for her date!

Wait. The perfume. She could not be ready without that final touch of tuberose. Yes. Now she felt complete. Strange, how the memories stole back to claim a place. She could plot a graph, with the memorable nodal points in their long association, going up and nose-diving. The exact events were difficult to extract from the web of memories, or the words exchanged, but she could distil the emotion that she had felt. The whiff of the perfume filled her with love, given and received.

She stepped out of her office, aware that she still commanded a second look. Well-rounded but not matronly, she had an elegance that bespoke her lineage. Mother of a daughter and a son, both married, Rupsa felt the light-headedness of an eighteen-year-old on her first date.

The nip in the air enhanced the whisper of romance. She walked light on her feet, heading for the cosy tea room in the corner bookshop, the venue for the date.

Ping ping. A message.

"C U in 10 minutes. Will be wearing a combination of brown. In eager anticipation. Roshan"

Fifty-six-year-old, five feet ten inches, salt and pepper hair, and with a crispness about him, Roshan could not concentrate on his work. Should he give her a rose? Perhaps a chocolate with it? Dark Fantasy? Rich and sensuous, to arouse the hormones.

"Stop. You're moving too fast. One step at a time," his inner voice chided him. He felt suitably chastened. With slow, deliberate movements, he put aside his files, cleared his table and checked his black, steel, slim watch. He remembered his first date and felt the same pangs of anticipation and excitement he had felt then, as a young college student. He felt light, free, and happy. Yes, pure unadulterated happiness. He had not experienced this in a long while. Time even then, had refused to move fast enough as he had waited at the University Special bus stop.

She had walked slowly towards him, a vision of blue and green. His heart had skipped a beat. Wafting ahead of her with the gentle breeze was a heady perfume. He soaked it in and felt giddy, then almost anaesthetised.

"Hi. So how was the tutorial?" he had mumbled for want of something more inspired to say and then had lovingly given her a hug.

He looked at his watch—4.45 pm. Time to move. He felt the cell phone buzz.

A message? Was it her? He was behaving like an impossible adolescent. Suppressing a smile, he checked his phone. "Will seek you out. I prefer corner tables :) Rupsa."

He had to move quickly if he was to grab the corner spot. The bookstore was a lively haunt, for the young and old alike. The young came to seek a dream, the old to revisit what seemed like a dream after so many years.

Tucked away in a quiet corner was the chai counter with a glass panel overlooking the busy road. You could watch the buzz and yet be far removed from it—enjoy the throb without the strain. The 'pick me up' was served in little earthen cups, and as an 'along', customers could choose from the display on the bamboo racks—spice cookies, raisin rock cakes, cheese sandwiches, and asparagus rolls. It was intimate without being claustrophobic.

Roshan moved with quick, confident steps. Yes, there was a corner table, with the understated lighting of the warm glow from the fragranced candle.

Roshan occupied the chair with the hint of a smile playing around his lips as he remembered the text message. The scent of the tuberose reached him before Rupsa did, and he felt his eyes drawn to her. "Had no problems locating you. You are Roshan, aren't you?" she was saying, her eyes laughing.

"Yes. Here I am. Welcome to your corner seat. You look just as I had imagined."

There. He had said it without spelling it out. Rupsa quickly took in the details of her date as they made themselves comfortable on the cane chairs with deep seats, high backs, and padded hand rests. "The man has taste, a kind of quiet class," she thought to herself. The beige trousers, off-white shirt, and jacket, in a slightly darker shade of brown, made him easy to look at. She particularly approved of the neat haircut, clean shaven, athletic appeal. "He takes care of himself and carries his age well," she thought.

"So what had you imagined?" she asked, holding his gaze.

"Well...," came his hesitant response, at a loss for words.

"Don't think so hard. Just say it, whatever is on your mind," she teased, enjoying his discomfort.

"You are just as you sound. Attractive and approachable..."

"But..."

"No. There is no 'but'. Instead, I could add a few more adjectives but I need to keep my restraint at the same time."

"Oh. Thank you. You built up an image from our conversations! Imagination can be deceptive and create unrealistic expectations. I may not be able to match up!"

She knew he wanted to know how she felt on meeting him, but wanted him to ask. Noticing his twinkling eyes and the smile lurking at the corners of his lips, she laughed aloud and said, "Okay. I will not keep you in suspense. You'll do!"

Roshan let out an exaggerated sigh of mock relief. "I was wondering whether I'd pass the acid test. This is worse than my first job interview!"

And so the two got talking, gently bantering, sharing, at ease without pretences, not trying too hard to impress each other, willing to talk about their little hurts, regrets, joys, and simple hopes and desires.

"So what was your first interview like?" asked Rupsa.

"Killing," came the spontaneous response, "She was a firm forty-five-year-old, with short, salt and pepper hair, quite a cat among the poor male pigeons, and I almost felt she could look right into my throbbing veins!"

"Quite the drama king, aren't you?" laughed Rupsa, at the graphic description and continued, "And, do you have any happiest moment?"

Roshan looked thoughtful and replied, "Moments. I would say there have been a few. Maxing my maths paper, a subject that always got my blood pressure high. Completing my first marathon. My first kiss, a little hesitant, but so full of passion and promise. Captaining my cricket team to victory. Becoming a father. Seeing my parents together on their fiftieth anniversary. Actually, this is the first time anyone has asked me this question. Let me put the question to you. Have you ever thought about it?"

"Yes," replied Rupsa, "purely as an academic exercise. I got it as an essay topic and I wrote what for me was most honest. The truth is, my happiest time was when I got the keys to my own apartment. The freedom was exhilarating. And then, I got a month all to myself. No gnawing questions, commitments, demands, schedules. I was with myself and my freedom. It sounds terribly selfish and pompous, perhaps, but I don't have to put up a front. However, I will add that the sheer thrill of freedom was precious at that point in time. Today, I feel comfortable with commitments, I miss not being asked questions."

Roshan nodded quietly, listening intently, "So, what made you come this evening? Was it curiosity, doing something different, taking a chance, what was it?"

Rupsa took a long sip of her iced tea and looked deep into his eyes. "What if I say I wanted to give myself another chance? I had become hard, suspicious, even insensitive. You sounded like someone I had once known and lost, who I could be myself with, have fun with, and who I could love without giving reasons for it. I hoped you wouldn't judge me too harshly. I hoped we could become friends."

The street lights had come on, and the aerial view of the dodging headlights created bizarre images. Roshan was pensive, introspective, thinking about what he was in search of at this stage of his life.

"Strange, isn't it, that after spending over twenty-five years together, we did not know each other's happiest moments. We had never asked each other," he said.

"For that matter, we don't know each other's greatest regrets or an unfulfilled desire that perhaps can see fruition in some way. When did we become strangers, Roshan?"

"Perhaps, when we started judging each other. You just said you were hoping not to be judged by me. Is that what you had felt?"

"I felt watched and blamed. I did not feel trusted. There seemed to be secrets and gradually, I felt that we were on parallel rails. I dreaded being abused with words that were far more lethal than a physical hit. There was anger and finally an ice cold pack. I had no spontaneity or laughter left in me. The pressure to be someone else was throttling. Occasionally, a station required us to alight and interact because of external demands but otherwise I had stopped expressing my feelings. There was no connect between us."

"We were meant to be meeting as strangers today. Ironically, that is the reality and no play acting. Even today I see the college student and can read her pulse; her half smile, the excitement bursting to be shared, the hurt pride hidden behind a translucent veil, the flirtatious gestures waiting to be responded to..."

"And then we see impenetrable walls which we cannot read. The people are the same at the core but there are too many layers that have corrupted the connection.

Remember the time when your uncle tried to get fresh with me? Actually it was on more than one occasion. I talked about this with your family but was told that it was a figment of my imagination. An over-reaction, from a supposed feminist. I felt humiliated and disrespected. As if I did not count and was not to be taken seriously. I did not belong to the family. I was lying about a real family member. That is how I experienced it.

I did not feel supported by you either, though you did not trivialise my problem like the others. It appeared to me that you were sitting safely on the fence. I felt alone and abandoned, like in the enemy camp, where I had to handle the situation by myself. Eventually, that camp became my safe island and I was fighting my battles alone."

The woman in front seemed far more at ease with herself. She had accepted herself. What stopped him?

Rupsa looked at Roshan and said, "What is stopping you from just saying what you feel? I can see a whole lot of unsaid thoughts and feelings running amuck. It's okay. You can talk about them."

Roshan thought aloud, "You know, I, too, had taken refuge inside my own fortress because I felt alone, rejected, not understood or cared for. I was merely the provider. It was like a clinical transaction. I was facing a lot of disappointments at work but there was no one I could share them with. No one I could turn to for comfort.

I lashed out, using words like spears, but they only violated me. I believed it would give me a sense of satisfaction, a high of winning my point, but ultimately, I was communicating with silence.

There were temptations of getting that companionship elsewhere but that was not what I was looking for either. I will not deny that I gave the opportunity some thought and time. It progressed a bit but probably my old fashioned morality came in the way.

I even wrote stories. Sometimes by fictionalising a situation, we find expression for the truth. It gives comfort, having released it."

"Yes, I realised that. I even read some of the stories that you deliberately kept lying around. This is the first time I have heard you disclose so much about yourself. So, what do you plan to do now, with all this learning and self-analysis? I did some digging myself, and realised I was taking everything too seriously and like a personal assault. That made me pretty obnoxious. My tunnel vision was making me see only the negatives and I was responding from there. You had your own demons to tackle. After our separation I could look at our relationship objectively and allow feelings that I had blocked."

"And?"

"And I did not want to severe it. I wanted to water all the green patches that had been neglected and turned barren. That had the promise of growing something beautiful. They gave me a lot of hope."

"You asked me what I plan to do now. I'll tell you what—if you ask me, let's just go back to that first memorable kiss and relive those moments again. Let us start by watering our first garden."

"Look, we are conversing, aren't we? It's so easy. Talking, like not in a debate, a cerebral battle of trying to make that winning point, but actually sharing our pain and hurt. There are many things that you said and I heard for the first time today, in all these years. We are having so much fun together also. Just relax and chill, as our twins would say."

"So, what is your greatest regret? Perhaps we could start with fixing that."

"There are a few, but for now, dancing the night away, with you, to begin with. Getting a little drunk and not bothering about what others say, or feeling judged."

"There is a pub nearby. They serve interesting stuff. We could even dance if you like the music. Does it sound inviting?"

"It sure does," was Rupsa's prompt response. "I have heard good reviews about it and the live band is very good. I would love to go."

Roshan felt the tension ebb as he let the soft music speak for them. The chilled beer and meat pie helped add to the enjoyment and the harmony that had settled in. It was past midnight when the two finally decided to call it a night. Sitting in the bedroom, Roshan turned to Rupsa and asked, "So, how about fixing our next date. Are you game?"

"I most certainly am," she replied, adding, "but only if you dance again like you did tonight, carefree, tension-free, holding me warm and close after nearly a decade."

Smiling a happy smile, highlighting his boyish charm, Roshan responded, "I will sweep you off your feet and prance around the room, but only if you wear the tuberose perfume again, the scent of your college days."

The next morning one excited voice called the marriage counsellor, "It actually worked, meeting like two strangers. We travelled back in time and found our lost bond. We talked, we danced, we romanced. We have even fixed our next date!"

The eastern sky had a tinge of colour, hinting at the promise of a new start. The marble gravestones in the old Kolkata cemetery gleamed in the fading moonlight. Two figures sat close together, holding hands.

"Rupsa, why didn't we go on that date when Mrs Singh asked us to? This is a regret I lived and died with. Not having given our marriage one more chance. How much fun we had together last night, dressing up, going to the cafe, dancing, and most importantly, talking. Really talking."

Rupsa was quiet for a few moments. "I actually forgot that it wasn't for real, that it wasn't happening in the world where we lived and breathed our last. My feelings are just as intense, Roshan. This *is* our second chance, maybe in another dimension, but we went on a date all right. My feet are still tired from all the dancing! And,

I still have so much left to say, to share that I know no one else will understand. Also, we both do not have any regret that we will carry, of letting our egos come in the way of our happiness."

"Come to think of it, we are now truly free to choose our date location, anywhere that we wish. There were so many places that we had on our bucket list that we had planned on visiting, once we had more free time. So, where should we go on our next date, Rupsa darling?"

"It's been ages since you called me that! We both loved listening to Eartha Kitt singing, 'Under the bridges of Paris with you, I'd make your dreams come true.' That was on our list. How about going on a leisurely boat ride there and living our dreams?"

As daylight broke, the cemetery became active with the caretaker and the gardeners getting on with their work. "There are no tuberoses planted in the cemetery but there is a strong aroma of the flower everywhere. I wonder where it is coming from?" said one gardener to the other.

6

Palash

"Palash, *niche esho.* Ma Baba *eshe gechen.*[1]" I was eleven years old. That was my grandmother calling me, urging me to go downstairs to greet my parents who had arrived from Germany. She could not understand my reluctance. Looking back, I know nobody really could—understand me, that is.

I knew they were to arrive that morning. Ganeshda had gone to the airport to receive them. To say that I was not excited would be a lie. I was. In fact, I was very curious about my younger sister whom I had not seen for a full year. She was eight years old.

"Palash, *babu tumi kothai*?[2]" That was my mother. I could hear her heels click as she came up the stairs. I came out of my room and she engulfed me in her soft, scented arms and showered me with kisses. She clung to me as I tried unsuccessfully to extricate myself. "Oh! How I have missed you! Don't run away." Stuck in the folds of her layers, I was feeling claustrophobic and tried to take a gasp of air in between her smothering. She wafted a spicy perfume that had marinated her being. It was the familiar breeze that I had once longed for as

---

[1] Come down, Palash, your parents have arrived.
[2] Palash, son, where are you?

a child when I drifted into the land where only dreams tiptoe. Innumerable nights I lay awake for that lullaby wind to stroke me with its invisible touch, to assure me that all was right with my world, when, in reality, it clearly wasn't.

"*Babu shona,* how you've grown in the past year. You reach up to my shoulder now. I have brought you a lot of things that little boys like you use in Germany. Seeing them enjoy these things, I was impatient to bring them for you. Why are you so quiet? Come, let us go and meet Baba and Bonti. They are waiting for you eagerly." The words ran into each other like a cascading waterfall with the little droplets panting to catch up. Feeling drops of guilt, regret, remorse, lament. Ahh! That insight made me feel better. I had little interest in investigating the bribe gadgets. They were as foreign and alien as those carrying them and I treated them with dollops of suspicion. But, who could I share this with?

I took a deep breath instead of Ma. I was unused to so much talk. Dadu and Didima were quiet people and the house was usually silent. Occasionally, my cousins Papri and Amitabha came over and for a few hours there would be some activity, friendly squabbles, and arguments over whether to order pepperoni or chicken pizza or biryani. The matter usually got sorted out with a benign bargain of each one getting the dish of his or her choice. The next day, I would look forward to devouring the leftovers from everyone else's item of choice.

That morning remains etched in my memory, deep in the crevasses of my amygdala. I was five then and can still sense the tension in the tissues—torn with resentment and fear, helplessness, and a feeling of rejection along with a stubborn (albeit naive) dash of hope and anticipation, in case minds changed. Why had I been cast off—denied the intimacy of my family? I was the older of the two siblings, the one who had come first into the lives of my parents, making us a cosy threesome. And yet, when my parents had to relocate to Germany for my father's job, I was considered too much of a burden to carry along. My two-year-old sister went with them. I never asked my parents the reasons behind their decision. Not that I was given a choice. The arrangement was merely conveyed to me. Apparently, or so I gathered from broken conversations, the reasons were my mother's inability along with her misgivings about managing two children on her own, without a maid, and the belief that I would be well looked after by my grandparents.

My father, utterly wedded to the betterment of his career and given the fortuitous opportunity of earning mega bucks overseas, agreed happily to the plan. It would ensure peace in his home abroad. He had no clue about nor the time for a mere five year old's queries and emotions. The boy, as far as he was concerned, would be adequately cared for.

No. I have no complaints against Dadu and Didima. They loved me. Perhaps to a fault and they tried to overcompensate. I never could get an answer to my unasked question. Would I have been that much of a trouble or a hindrance to their carefree life in Europe? Did they not miss me? I had joined school in Kolkata and then the logic was that they would be coming back in three years' time. I would have a hard time adjusting to the rigours of Indian education when I got back. And so, I remained separated from them for six years.

My grandparents attended the parent-teacher meetings and I became an object of curiosity and analysis. "Actually, he has been kept here to get disciplined." "No, no, the real story is something entirely different. It is to do with a family secret. I have been told by reliable sources." "Actually his mother does not want to be seen tagging along a grown child. He is an embarrassment. She was known for getting younger every year." The rumours and stories became more robust and my resistance to them increasingly anaemic. Young though I was, I was neither oblivious nor impervious to this slander and I retreated into the safety of my own skin shell.

There were my annual summer vacation visits to Germany and their winter trips to Kolkata. I would see my sister going to her fun school in Germany and I often longed for the experience myself, stuck as I was in the rigid system in India with sixty to a class where I was just a number, not being particularly dynamic in any way. A grain strewn and forgotten in the sands of mediocrity. My growing years were lost to them and along with it, my soul. They remained distant relatives for me.

Finally, they relocated to Kolkata and I became the tailwind, supporting them in their readjustment to the challenges of life in the city stuck in time. I couldn't help but feel that I was one of the major challenges being tackled. It took me many months to become a son instead of a grandson—the demands, expectations were all so different. Etiquette and manners were the new concerns for me. I needed to be smartened up and made worthy of my parents, returned from a foreign land. More at home with the genial, affectionate, and laidback company of my grandparents' generation, I was unused to the scrutiny in the prying eyes of my parents' acquaintances. Trying desperately to reclaim the slippery foothold on the societal ladder, I was an important crutch for my parents. The ideal progeny.

It happened on a December Friday night, a few years later. I was eighteen. The temperature had dipped to a chill. "Let me see you, Palash," my mother said with a hint of disappointment that I was getting used to and also very conscious of. "You must be smart and sparkling. After all, you are *my* son. There will be guests tonight who are all very fashionable and stylish. You must not mumble when they ask you something. Answer them confidently and don't slouch."

"Not presentable enough in front of her champagne froth. Well, I'll show her," I said to myself. Something, somewhere had snapped inside me and I wanted to hit back. I could feel the feeling billowing into an unstoppable surge. Filling up my chest, throat, face, and head.

"You will be meeting them after many years. Spriha will be coming too. Remember, how you looked forward to the gifts she brought you when you were a child?" my mother continued.

Spriha Mashi[3]. The oh-so-attractive and desirable friend of my mother. I had always suspected my mother of being secretly jealous of her, having neither her charm nor her spirited attitude. Spriha Mashi was a young

---

[3] Maternal aunt.

widow who had lived through a dull and listless marriage and always seemed to be searching for that spark and loving companionship. The flammable memory was ignited and a fire crept through my veins. Of course, I remembered. Not just the gifts but much more. It was a still afternoon and my parents were not home during one of their winter breaks in Kolkata. Slender, scented Spriha Mashi in her trousers and well-fitted unbuttoned shirt, lay entwined with an uncle, a close family friend, on the sofa. Even as a nine year old, I remember my pulse racing wildly and I couldn't take my eyes off the alluring apparition in front of me. Startled at seeing them, I must have made a sound because I remember her awkward laugh as she came to me and said, "Hello, Palash. I have something special for you." And she delved into her chic black bag and retrieved a G.I. Joe. Somehow, even then I knew that what I had witnessed could not be disclosed to anyone.

The guests started streaming in, the music got drowned in tinkling conversation and the clink of wine glasses and the spirits started taking effect. I had gulped down a couple in quick succession and the world was a haze of heady perfumes and unedited conversation. I had taken care to dress for the occasion. A dark blue, slim fit shirt that sat fairly nicely, I thought, on my gym toned arms and torso and a pair of well-cut, slate grey trousers. The barber had done a good job with the close crop and a splash of Obsession added the final touch. I felt good and upbeat. Free in a strange dreamlike sort of way. In the mood to take risks.

It was Spriha Mashi who first came up to me and said, "Palash, I've been watching you. What a handsome young man you've grown into. I want you to be my partner in the next dance."

Me, handsome! In the eyes of the elegant, scintillating, enticing Spriha Mashi! My ripening blood sped through my groins. It was an enchanted few minutes after that as I put my arms around her, holding her close, trying to guide her on the crowded dance floor. "Let's go to the balcony, Mashi," I ventured as the music changed. She agreed readily and I could sense the urgency in her too.

Under the dark, star studded sky, in the chilled, crisp night air and with the half-moon as our witness, we locked warm, eager lips. That seemed the most natural course of things. It was a moment of exhilaration for me. My lungs felt like they would burst and my heart took on a new life. I was a man with charm, etiquette, and manners, good enough to sweep the femme fatale of the evening off the floor. For as long as I could remember, my mother had always tried to mould herself to the standards set by Spriha. And today, she wanted me.

And so began our clandestine meetings. We were the odd couple one could say but I cannot explain my sense of thrill and fulfilment. I completed graduation and was soon absorbed in a company known to Spriha. She encouraged me in my aspiration to do an MBA, which I did along with the job. I had dropped the 'mashi' long ago and it was a huge effort keeping up pretences when we met in front of my family.

It was obviously a dreadful shock when I declared to my parents that I was going to marry Spriha. Disbelief, a look of complete betrayal, hurt, and sheer pain flashed across their faces. "How could you?" whispered Ma in a hoarse voice.

"Yes, Ma, I can and I will," I answered with a firm ring, adding, "The question now is, how could *you*?"

"How could I what? What have we done that made you do this? Is this some form of revenge? We have always only had your best interests at heart," she replied.

I looked at them hard for a while and then asked in a slow deliberate pace, "Did you ever ask me, what was best for me? Have you ever put yourself in my place and thought of what it felt like, being cast aside from the family unit like a pariah? You were both busy just thinking of your convenience. Would you like to know how I felt? Even if you don't, let me tell you. I felt I had done something wrong. It was as if I was not good enough or important enough for the two of you. I felt as if I was a mistake in your lives that you have been trying to correct all this while."

The outpouring was an explosion of all the 'uns' buried deep inside me—unloved, unspoken, unaccepted, ungiven, unasked, unwanted, unforgiven. The bitter corrosive feelings that had corrupted my guts. And then, I wept the unshed emotions. Hot, stinging tears of relief, deep sorrow and finally, strangely enough, peace and tranquillity. The tremors of violent sentiments gradually subsided and in the silence that followed, Ma and Baba sank into the sofa with what sounded like a traumatised sigh, not knowing how to respond. Then my father spoke, "Believe us when we say we did not understand what you were going through. We are so so sorry. But, why this? Why punish yourself by marrying her?"

"Spriha is my friend. How can she be your wife? Besides, I know her well. She will use you and then cast you aside. She is just doing it to prove a point about her capability of trapping a young man even at her age. She is also trying to spite me in some way. Besides, think of what a social scandal it will be. Think of your family. You are playing with your life. What will it get you? How will this disastrous decision help you?" my mother lamented with a note of hysteria.

"You still don't get it, do you?" I whispered. "It has always been all about you. I am doing myself a huge favour for the first time. This will be my closure, my healing for the wound that has festered all these years. Other than the fact that Spriha made me feel like a man who is needed and loved for who and what I am, when you both see us together, you will always get reminded of the son you could have had...."

7

The Mango Orchard

In the sterilised ambience of the supermarket, the shoppers went about in a crisp and business-like manner, robotically pulling things off the shelves and dunking them into the trolley. Mala, too, merged with the crowd. There were moments when she still missed the human touch. She had always enjoyed her outings with her mother to the local market in Kolkata. On her trips back home, she made a point of going to the market at least once to top up on nostalgia until her next visit. In Manhattan, there was no one to answer inane questions like, "Is it fresh? Just two days ago it cost five rupees less per kilogram. How can you overcharge like this? Pintu, the boy just down the lane, has a much better selection of fruits. Why don't you improve your quality?" There was no scope for a little benign haggling or a shopkeeper offering a cup of hot tea in an earthen cup, "*Bhalo cha, didi. Khan. Hebby taste.*[1]" No affectionate comments like, "*Didi, besh to chilen, eto roga kyano hoye gelen? Shob thik toh?*[2]" These were the touches of her city, not on any fast track to super quick development, but quite content ambling along, observing the world at large.

---

[1] Good tea, sister. Drink it. Great taste.

[2] You were fine, sister. Why have you lost so much weight? Is everything all right?

Mala Seth was a name to reckon with in that exclusive club of investment bankers on the street that called the shots. New York was the place to be, and that was where she had been for the past twelve years. Ruthlessly ambitious, she had shattered the glass ceiling in her company, and blazed an inferno of a trail. She had an intuitive skill for taking calculated risks and making a success of her high profile clients' businesses. Anyone who posed a challenge to her career moves was quickly and efficiently dealt with and would never make the mistake of crossing her path again.

She followed the man in front of her, carefully manoeuvring her trolley in the aisle between the shelves stacked with baked munchies. At thirty-five, she needed to be all the more conscious of what went into her body.

"Your metabolic rate will slow down, so be aware of the calories you put in, and make sure of how much you work out in the week. You slack off now and you can feel the flab all over," her personal trainer had warned her.

'Slack off '—the words were not in her dictionary. No slacking off in her exercise regime, no popping in that inviting tiramisu, no respite from her all-consuming job, no letting down her guard at work. The economy was slack and to hold her post she had to compensate by placing more demands on herself.

No relaxing, not even in her marriage. She had to make a success of it as well. She was a winner, wasn't she?

She had met Dinesh a couple of years ago. He was an IT professional and was quite smitten by her 'aloof appeal', as he put it. Later, in their more intimate moments, he had confessed, "I could sense the fire under the ice and was dying to stoke it."

"And, what if the flames get out of control—can you handle that?" she had teased.

"Why don't you test me out? But then I will not be responsible for the consequences," he had challenged.

And so they had tumbled from the bed to the carpet, and Mala's regulated life had gone for a toss, temporarily. A happy toss, she thought, as she relived the moments.

Living in the US, she had all the independence she wanted. Financially she was more than secure, she needed companionship and her in-laws lived far away in India and so there would be no shadow on her freedom. Dinesh was not particularly demanding in any way and seemed to accept her decision to not have a child anytime soon. "We can always adopt if we want to at a later stage. I am sorry, but right now I don't have the luxury to take any time off from my taxing schedule. Going off the grid even for a few months will push me back many steps," she told him when he had brought up the subject. Unwilling to get into a debate, Dinesh realised he had two choices, either to accept or opt out of the marriage. For the time being, he was willing to play along. Besides, having Mala as his wife, had its advantages too.

She had reached the end of the aisle and turned right to stock up on fresh fruits. Apart from the usual apples, bananas, grapes, melons, and berries, Mala saw the mangoes and her heart skipped a beat. They sat there, bursting with an appeal all of their own. Mala walked up, caressed one tenderly, brought it to her nose, breathing the sweet aroma until it satiated her. There was a hunger in her touch, an agitation in her senses, and a deep feeling of inexplicable sadness. Inexplicable? Not quite.

Brushing aside her feelings almost brusquely, she blindly put some fruits into the trolley and then unable to resist herself, put in four juicy mangoes, despite the exorbitant price tag.

Walking out quickly from the shop, she pushed her trolley to the car and unloaded her purchases. Almost unconsciously, she ensured that the mangoes were right on top, to prevent them from getting pressed and squeezed.

That night it was a quiet and introspective Mala who sat for dinner with Dinesh. "These mangoes are delicious. It reminds me of home. A pity we get such few varieties here," remarked Dinesh.

"Yes," agreed Mala, "I miss the innumerable flavours. Baba's *bagaan bari*[3] has an orchard with such a huge variety of mango trees. He picked them up from all over." And then, on an impulse, she added, "You know, I think I'll go to Kolkata on a short trip. My leave is due and I could do with a break. Besides, this is the mango season!" Dinesh was surprised. Mala was never given to impulses but he agreed with her. He had noticed that she had been pushing herself too hard and needed to unwind.

Packing for a trip back home was always a challenge. There were so many things she wanted to take. Though now, unlike a few years earlier, practically everything

---

[3] Garden house.

was available in India, yet it was special if she carried it with her. Cheeses, special savouries, unusual sauces, fruit preserves, good perfumes, creams and toiletries, medicine containers for her parents to store the pills they needed for the week, good winter wear, clothes, chocolates, and this time she also picked up two high quality stethoscopes. "You don't need to carry so many things, Mala Ma," her father would say, but she could see the joy and excitement on his face as he received his gifts. "You always get my favourite perfume," her mother would say with a happy smile as she munched on a cracker topped with various seeds. Her brothers would be hovering around her like eager little children, as she unpacked their special presents.

The trip to Kolkata was long and tedious. International flights to the city were limited and she took one with a layover in the Middle East. Space was cramped on the plane and there were noisy kids who insisted on running along the aisle, strewing the floor with empty packets of chips and crispies. There were a few complaints that fell on deaf ears. The parents were far too busy on the entertainment channels and had forsaken all responsibilities.

Mala watched a movie for a while and then switched off from her immediate surroundings. She was tired—fatigued by the race and the goals she had set for herself. It was lonely up there and she was unsure if anybody genuinely cared for her. Soon, she lost herself in the comforting reverie of especially the last two summers of her school years. Her father's *bagaan bari*, spread over several acres, was an hour and a half's drive from

Kolkata. Every summer vacation, the family would migrate there, except her father, who would join them on the weekends. Her two younger brothers, her mother, and she would relax together, bathing in the pond, drinking fresh coconut water, and munching on freshly roasted puffed rice spiced with chopped onions, green chillies, diced coconut, peanuts, a dash of mustard oil, and salt.

And then there was Raja, the gardener's son. A year older to Mala, he was a strapping young lad, mild mannered, a storehouse of stories, great fun to be with. He studied in the local government school with promising results. He hoped to go to the city for higher studies. Becoming a doctor was his ambition and he dreamed of serving the villagers.

Mala had spent hours in his company, even as a young girl, and was enthralled by his stories from Indian mythology, especially the *Ramayana* and the *Mahabharata*. "Imagine the plight of Sita or Draupadi. They may be revered but I would never want to be in their shoes. Caught in the tentacles of societal demands, their lives were so controlled," observed a rebellious Mala.

"Oh, I am certain that our epics would have had a different storyline had you been the female protagonist, even in those times. You would probably have jumped out of the story and demanded that the incidents be rewritten if you were feeling curbed!" teased Raja. And they laughed heartily, recreating the episodes from the mighty epics according to what suited their sensibilities and their reality.

He taught her to climb trees, especially the mango and guava ones. "Look at the ripe *himsagar*[4] on that branch at the top. I dare you to get it for me," said Mala, peering longingly at the delicious fruit.

"You won't be able to trap me with your challenges," replied Raja with an all knowing smile. "You want it, go get it. I am standing right here and will catch you if you fall but both of us know that you won't. You just need to be a little brave."

"Are you calling me a coward? Don't think that I can't get it without your help," replied Mala, playing right into his hands. He knew that to question her fierce sense of independence or her spirit was the ideal way to get her to achieve a difficult task. And so, the next few moments saw a nervously determined barefoot young girl, clamber on to the tree, gripping the branches firmly while placing her feet with care, until she got her prize. She sat herself down on a thick branch at a fork in the tree, resting her back on another branch with her legs dangling and gorged on the fruit, bursting with sweet victory flavours. Then, feeling a twinge of guilt, she plucked another one and dropped it for Raja to have too.

They would sit in the cool mango orchard and polish off kilos of the fruit, relishing the variety. "If you plant the mango seed, after some time when you take it out I can make a whistle for you," he promised her. Tired of ripe mangoes, they would sometimes pluck the raw ones. He would shave off the skin and crush the pulp, adding

---

[4] A type of mango, native to Bengal. It is known for its thin skin, golden hue, sweet aroma, unparalleled sweetness, and complete lack of fibres.

sugar, green chillies, and rock salt to make a tangy relish that she would save up to have with her food or to suck on, making a clicking sound with her tongue when the sour taste tickled.

He was also her fishing instructor. She remembered her excitement when she caught her first fish in the pond but was too scared to pull it out, and a laughing Raja helped her heave up the prize catch. It was a thrilling moment but the slippery creature kept jumping around and she couldn't bear to watch it gasping. "Let it go, let it go," she cried with a hint of desperation. Seeing her, Raja immediately released the fish back into the water, much to her relief. "Thank you, thank you," she sobbed, holding on to Raja for comfort. "It's all right. It's safe in its home," he assured her, instinctively understanding and responding to the softer core inside her.

Sitting in her seat on the plane, Mala felt the fresh joy and happiness that she had not experienced in a long while. No pretences, nothing to prove, just the sheer comfort of understanding each other and enjoying each other's company. This deep friendship slowly bloomed into the blush of first love. It took Mala a while to understand it and moreover to accept it. But, she also knew that the emotion could only be felt and cherished, never expressed. The same Mala, who had objected to the lives of Sita and Draupadi, when faced with a hard decision, succumbed to the unwritten norms of her society. And, so began her tryst with covering up her true feelings. This match would be unacceptable to both families and Mala knew her father would not survive the shock.

Sensitive Raja could see the change in her behaviour. He had loved her as a chubby girl, eagerly soaking in his stories and being his ever willing pupil. As she matured into a lady, he loved her even more but respected her far too much to make advances. He knew that she would be going abroad for further studies after completing her graduation. In that last summer of her Class XII, as they sat under the mango grove, he told her, "I don't know when we will meet after today but my summers will never be the same. Come. Let me show you something."

He took her to a plot of land that his father had bought for him.

"This is my land. I will plant a mango orchard here. It will be ours. And, for every summer after you leave, I will plant a new mango sapling in memory of our times together. When you visit, you must come here and taste some of the mangoes, and think of me when you have the juiciest ones," he said with a sad smile, aware that he could not fight the circumstances.

Mala could barely stand there while he spoke. With tears flowing down her cheeks, she held on to his hands, and then clung to him, her tears drenching his shirt. "I wish I actually had the guts to be the heroine that you thought I would be. My life will never be the same again and I will miss you so very much." Saying this she turned around and ran back to the house. She fleetingly met him a few more times while she was studying for her graduation and he was in medical school, and then she left for the US.

Mala reached Kolkata to be greeted by her excited family. After all the hugging and kissing they went home and she walked into the solace of her room. It was the one place that had not changed, much like the core inside her. Her books, bed, easy chair, music, and photo albums were kept the way she had placed them. Even her book of poetry in which she had scribbled her unvoiced thoughts and feelings was there in her cupboard.

Conversation over dinner revolved around all of the family gossip; who was going around with whom, whose kids were doing what, who had said what and why… Mala's younger brother, who was earning his MD, said, "Didi, do you remember Raja? He is an MD, has set up a clinic in the village, and is collaborating with some individuals to expand it into a small hospital. He has plans of building a hostel, so that doctors can stay on the premises, and hopes to get some specialists to visit so that the local people get quality healthcare. I will be going day after, why don't you come along to the *bagaan bari*?"

"That would be wonderful!" exclaimed Mala, feeling false in her reaction but experiencing a burst of joy and pride within her.

She found it difficult to hide her excitement.

Memories of bygone summers tiptoed into all her free moments. Hesitantly at first and then with more confidence they strode into her busier times also, making her distracted and impatient for the proposed visit. Feelings, long suppressed and 'unvisited', overwhelmed her. How was he? Was he married? Did he remember their orchard? The questions flew through her mind with an urgency and intensity beyond her control. To quell her excitement and agitation, she made a visit to the nursery from where her parents always bought plants.

Greens had a soothing impact on her and she spent a while looking around and made some purchases that brought her pure joy.

The family excursion was made and when everyone had retired for a long summer afternoon siesta, Mala took a walk by herself to 'their' orchard, unsure of what to expect. This was her first visit to the promised haven since her class XII summer. On reaching her destination, she looked up hesitantly. Her heart was crushed with unexpressed emotions. There, in front of her, were twelve mango trees in various stages of growth. The thirteenth one had been freshly planted.

Mala walked up slowly and kept the bag that she was carrying, very carefully, next to her. She then took out twelve mango saplings of twelve different varieties that she had bought from the nursery and started planting them.

"I somehow knew I'd find you here. Your brother mentioned that you would be visiting today. How have you been?"

The familiar voice was like a spark to her rusted internal ignition. With a small gasp, she turned around and faced the gentle smile of *her* Raja. He had filled out a little and there was a quiet confidence about him. He was still wearing his doctor's coat.

"I have just completed my clinic hours and your brother has taken over. He is a big help," said Raja, all the while looking at her very keenly.

For once, the all sure Mala was at a loss for words. "You planted thirteen mango trees. You kept your promise," she said in a rush.

"I did. You look a little sad. Aren't you happy to find them growing well? Some of them are bearing fruit as well. I get news of your New York life from your brother. He says you are very successful at your work and your husband too is a good person. Congratulations!" responded Raja.

Avoiding all conversation relating to her personal life, and looking deep into his eyes, she said, "I'm so happy for you. You are slowly achieving all that you set out to do. So many people will be benefitted. I am very proud of you. You must be feeling very contented and peaceful doing all this."

"And you? Why do I get the feeling that you are not satisfied with your life? You found it all, the life that you chose. I had hoped that you would come here to visit me but then I understood that this life would not challenge you, would not be exciting enough, which it truly isn't. I really missed you, Mala, and distracted myself with studies and trying to set up a hospital here. Getting funds, permissions, and doctors is thankfully time consuming and soon the months rolled into years and I found closure. It was not easy but I kept myself busy. When I heard that you were visiting today, I had to come and see you."

Unable to hold back her burning tears, Mala realised that while Raja had found closure, she had actually embarked on a fresh chapter, linked to the continuation of her past. Her search for what was meaningful to her had only just begun, perhaps a little too late. "I was lost. Yes, I have done well, very well and it brings me some satisfaction too but there is no one to share it with. I don't want all that anymore, Raja. Can we please go back and start again? I have lost what was most important to me. I want companionship, laughter, and tears, teasing and missing...learning and sharing... I have missed all of this and become metallic...without feeling the variation in temperatures or touch...."

The gentle doctor, perhaps the only one who understood where she was coming from and where she was headed, held her hands in a warm clasp and said, "You are a determined person, Mala. You will find your way forward. At least, now you know what you are looking for. You are listening to your heart. But for us, we have our memories and our mango orchard. When I understood that you had made a choice, I made mine. I too got married and we have a baby daughter. I have named her Malama."

8

Unfinished

I have to admit that I have a fixation for finishing things and not leaving a job incomplete. "If you start something, make sure that you complete it," is a command that still rings in my ears, so many decades later. A life lesson I learnt from my father. I also need to know how something ended, the culmination, even if I did not start it. In fact, anything incomplete bothers me to the point of twitchiness. A clinical assessment would, in all likelihood, label me with an OCD diagnosis, Obsessive Compulsive Disorder.

An almirah partially cleaned, a hedge half trimmed, utensils washed and not dried and put away, a phone call with no voice on the other end, a bed in the process of being made and then abandoned in the morning, a story left incomplete...the list is endless. The problem is that this bee that buzzes in my bonnet does not stay contained within just my beginnings and endings. It encroaches into the lives of others around me, their incomplete business, and then proceeds to buzz in my brain. Zzzzzzz...it goes till I am quite beside myself until a solution is found or a 'finished' button is pressed.

So this is what happened. There was a wedding in the family, and everyone had gathered in Lucknow, at my grandparents' old-fashioned bungalow named Mukherjee

Villa. As is the norm these days, the younger generation were all making their way from across the globe to meet up for what promised to be a family reunion of a mega kind. Second cousins were meeting each other for the first time, first cousins were greeting each other in person after more than a decade. Most had expanded, a few had contracted, there were streaks of white, entirely grey for the braver individuals, while manes were dyed burgundy, black or even a combination!

There were dollops of nostalgia and old family tales in the conversations, updates on the major events in each other's lives, relaxation in the comfort of old familiar faces and surroundings, unlimited rounds of tea and snacks, and endless trips to the bazaar. The *chikankari* work that Lucknow is famous for had many takers. "I just have to take back saris, salwar suits, table and bed linen with this gorgeous embroidery. The pastel shades, the floral motifs, the subtlety and elegance are quite unmatched. And now they are embellishing it with pearl and mirror," gushed my cousin Minnie who had flown in from the United States. Others saved up their appetites for the juicy kebabs, *sheermal*[1], and the delicious biryani, topped off with *kulfi*[2], while the youngsters, uninitiated into the wonders of the heritage city, wanted to wander off into the mysteries of the *bhool bhulaiya* or the architectural maze, for which Lucknow is well known.

The senior-most members of the family, who lived in the house, were my father's eldest brother who was

[1] A saffron-flavoured flatbread.

[2] A frozen dessert made with thickened, flavoured milk and nuts.

ninety-two and his wife who was eighty-five. I had always been interested in history as a subject and my current fascination was our own family history. Our records went back to the sixteenth century and I had been trying to put together a volume with names, pictures, and whatever stories I could gather. To help me in my project, my uncle had given me some invaluable inputs through personal diaries, which had been found in the treasure trove of the library in the house. It was difficult to maintain the books and protect them from pests. Many of them had been donated to the state library for archival purposes but the diaries were personal to the family.

It was a summer wedding, and the family gathered in the large, open courtyard of the single-storied house. To relive old memories, it was decided that everyone would sleep on the charpoys of the bygone era, under the stars. For some, the experience was entirely novel. Standing fans had been arranged, little mosquito repellent devices had been installed, the floor of the cement courtyard had been washed to cool off the heat of the day, and as the shadows lengthened there was the stirring of a balmy breeze. The corners of the courtyard had small earth patches where flowering trees were in bloom. The gentle wind brought with it the fragrance of the white summer flowers. It was a practice amongst many of us to shower before going to bed, especially in summer, to wash off the day's fatigue and prepare the mind and body to welcome the soothing whisperings of the long night. The natural aroma of the flowers eased out any remaining stressors. As the chatter of the family quietened with drowsy eyes, one could hear the whistle of the long distance trains, calling out to those willing to listen. It evoked in me a strange, wistful, inexplicable feeling, of a loved one going far away into the dark unknown, with unconvincing promises of ever returning again. I remember the night clearly.

There was a full moon. The silver ball was playing hide and seek with the billowy clouds in the velvety sky and the courtyard was aglow in the white ethereal light. As I lay on my back, I could see the silhouette of the terrace in the pale moonlight. The silence of the shadows had fallen like a hush, and I gazed up, trying to decipher the constellations we had learnt as children—The Great Bear, Orion's Belt. As I scanned the sky eagerly for other star formations, my eyes caught a strange sight. Was I seeing things? Was I asleep? Just to be sure, I called out softly to my cousin sleeping next to me, "Minnie, can you see something on the terrace?"

In a soft, slightly scared tone, Minnie responded, "I've been meaning to ask you, but somehow I felt it was my imagination. Yes, I've been noticing the figure in white standing at the edge of the terrace. Somehow, I think the figure looks very sad, something about the way the shoulders are drooping."

Assured that it was not a figment of my mind, we spoke to each other in hushed tones about what or who it could be. "It looks like a woman going by the body structure, though it is unclear. Also, it almost appears to be floating. Am sure it is supernatural but it doesn't frighten me. Perhaps because we are all here together," commented Minnie.

Agreeing with her I added, "I wonder if it is there every night or is here just now, since the whole family has congregated. Do you think it is one of our ancestors?" Neither of us was convinced we believed in spirits, ghosts or apparitions, never having encountered one before. But we had read enough descriptions of them, from those who claimed to have seen them. Unable to reach a logical conclusion, we finally drifted into a fitful sleep, with unanswered questions swirling around in our heads.

Not desirous of causing panic and yet eager to find an answer to who our nocturnal visitor was, we went on an investigative mission the next morning. Seeking out Ramu Chacha, who had been with the family for several decades, we took him aside and confided our observations to him. He listened patiently and answered, "It is Lila Didi you saw. The story goes back to a time when you were not even born. Lila Didi was the daughter of the house. She was a beautiful, accomplished lady who happened to fall in love with the son of the family Dewan. This was just not acceptable to the family elders, and they sent the boy away. But the story did not end there. The two were committed to each other, and refused to marry anyone else. They kept in touch, somehow or other. Finally, their unfinished story ended tragically with both of them taking their lives together, when Lila Didi was being forced into a marriage of the family's choice. They knew there was no escape for them since her father was an influential man and would hunt them out."

The story struck a chord in our hearts. Lila Didi was our ancestor, after all, and she had not found peace even in death. As I mentioned, I have a fetish for things unfinished.

The diaries! Intuitively, I felt that the diaries would give me some more information. As I had expected, one of the diaries was that of Lila Didi. She spoke to her diary as her most trusted friend and had recorded her feelings, apprehensions, disappointments, dreams, and her decisions. She had kept the diary well hidden in her room. It had been discovered by my uncle fairly recently when the house was getting renovated. I read the diary through the whole day. I will share an excerpt.

I have given him a name which only I have the privilege to call him by. Khas. He actually is the embodiment of the name since he is so special. As usual, we met on the terrace today and he held me in a way he has never done earlier, almost like he wanted to make me dissolve into his being. To be honest, I felt a little alarmed. Quite soon it was clear that my apprehensions were not unfounded. My father had appointed a spy to keep an eye on me and news of our meetings has reached him. He is furious and has decided to send Khas away to manage our estate in Bengal, miles away from me....

There are things that I know about my father that I am sharing only with you. It is shameful and I cannot even tell my mother. She is too fragile to handle it. Besides, she will not believe me. I know why he is against our union. I overheard him talking to Khas's mother. He has had an affair with her and she has a child, a daughter, whose father is actually my father. Her husband, the dewan, does not know this either.

Khas, it is not our problem that our parents are cheating on their spouses.

I finally shared this information with Khas and he has been in shock. He thinks that perhaps it is best that he goes away.

We are both so distraught. There can be no one else in my life other than him. Of that I am sure…

Now that Khas is not here, I am allowed a little more freedom to step out of the house. A friend of mine from college, is running a school for the children of the prostitutes, who live in a house run by a brothel madam. She has rich clients for her lady escorts, but their children are not accepted by the society. My father, when he found out that I was teaching there, was livid, but I stuck to my ground. Do you know how? I found the courage to tell him that I knew his secret and you should have seen his expression! The other reason I go to my friend is because Khas sends letters to her address for me. So we can be in touch…

This evening, some people had come over. I realised that the pressure to marry someone else is becoming impossible and unbearable. I don't see any future to my life the way I would like it. Khas is also feeling the same way. He is in Lucknow and will be coming over to talk to our parents. We are determined…

I have been kept locked up in the house and there is a guard all the time to keep an eye on me. Apparently, the marriage date has been fixed with the boy who had come over. He comes from a rich family and I will not be surprised if it is a business deal of some kind that my father has entered. He has run into a lot of debts with his gambling. My mother came to convince me to accept the situation, and said that everything would work out once I got married. I pity her condition. She has lived her entire life like a doormat. I am so angry, I feel like screaming but who will listen to me. Maybe there is something else we can do to shut them up forever…

We saw her again that night, a lost, desolate figure, walking a lonely walk, trying to reach out to us for help. Reading the diary had made me all the more determined to do something for her. She deserved better. I was curious about how she had managed to escape and meet Khas, before the two ended their lives. Once again Ramu Chacha filled in the gaps. "A couple of days before the wedding, Lila Didi had been invited by her mother's sister for lunch. She managed to escape from there and went to her friend's place. From what I was told, Khas met her there and they both consumed a lethal poison because they felt there was no hope of them being together."

Taking Minnie into confidence along with Ramu Chacha, I decided to give an ending to the unfinished affair, a happy ending.

Call it madness or an act of compassion, we took the help of a priest and arranged a wedding ceremony on the terrace. On the following day we secretly decorated a small *mandap*[3] with flowers and all the wedding paraphernalia. The *purohit*[4] was roped into our plan, and we made him swear to complete secrecy, for a fee, of course.

We did not forget the feasting either! Minnie and I informed the family that we would be organising the dinner that night and we did, with biryani, kebabs, different varieties of rotis, some lentils and vegetables, and of course *shahi tukra*,[5] and *kulfi* as the finishing touch. It was after all a family wedding, even if a little

---

[3] Place where a Hindu marriage or puja is held.
[4] Priest.
[5] A dessert made with bread, sugar, thickened milk, and nuts.

unconventional, and no Indian wedding is complete without a sumptuous meal. We even laid out some food on the terrace.

Sure that the family had safely retired for the night, we crept up to the terrace, and the priest started the wedding rituals.

The mantras echoed softly as they seemed to be released into the vast universe to seek out the troubled souls. We had laid out two floral garlands. The god of fire was ignited to help them take the *saptapadi*, seven sacred steps, and we had even placed wedding attires for the couple. Minnie had bought them and of course they had *chikankari* work on them!

It was a strange yet enchanting sight for anyone who may have chanced upon us. The priest, the mantras, the fire, the audience, were all present and, we fervently hoped the spirit of the two souls in love, who we prayed would finally find peace. It had been a long wait for them, across decades.

The *purohit* continued to chant the mantras in all earnestness and sincerity, occasionally kindling the fire with ghee. He even paused a bit in between his chanting, when the couple is supposed to do the necessary actions. And then, at that pristine moment, when the darkest hour eases into the beginnings of a new dawn, the melody of birdsong came to our ears. Minnie and I held hands tightly as our eyes fell upon two white birds, perched on a branch overhanging the terrace. It was not common to see birds at that time and these two had a magical appeal to them. They exuded a glow, and appeared to be fully involved in the ceremony. The universe had responded to our call, sought out the soul-mates, and brought them to us.

They were sitting contentedly together, singing in harmony, repeating what we were both convinced, the wedding vows.

9

Refuge

Excitement blew through the historic *rajbari*[1], shooing away even the slightest hint of depression that may have lurked in some cobwebbed corner. It aired the minds and bodies of all the inhabitants, young and old, and brought them to their feet, to prepare for the homecoming. There were innumerable things to do, from the *alpona*[2] to the cleaning of the huge cooking utensils for preparation of the *bhog*[3]; the buying of all the puja ingredients; choosing the *dhaki*[4]; stocking the grocery. The *thakur dalan*[5] got a fresh coat of paint and the *pukur*[6] next to it had eager eyes peering into it, to see if the *rui machch*[7] were big enough to meet the family demands.

Everyone in Madan's house, too, was eagerly awaiting Ma Durga's autumnal ten-day visit. This year the clay idol was being modelled in the premises of the *rajbari*. This

---

[1] A mansion or palace built as a residence for an aristocrat, typically in Bengal.

[2] Designs on the floor made with a thin paste of ground rice.

[3] Food offered to the deities.

[4] Drummer.

[5] Place where the idol of the deity is kept.

[6] Pond.

[7] River carp.

added to the excitement and involvement of everyone living there, including the staff and the greater family. The *potua*[8] had been provided a room and he worked tirelessly, to sculpt the perfect pose of the goddess, slaying the demon *Mahishashur*[9]. This signified the victory of good over evil. He also made the clay models of her children and her carrier, the lion.

Ma Durga brought with her hope and cheer and, of course, new clothes, slippers, good food, and good money. Madan's thirteen-year-old son whispered enthusiastically to his father, "Raja Babu is giving all of us five shirts each, two pairs of trousers, a sweater, and a set of kurta and pyjama."

Raja Raj Bahadur loosened his purse strings, at this time of the year. This year in particular, he was being more generous. It was the seventy-fifth year of the puja celebrations in the family. It had to be a grand affair. Celebrities had been invited from the city. His societal status had to be reaffirmed with the scale of the celebrations!

Madan looked at all their faces and wished he could share their joy. A month earlier, he had been called by the Raja. "This time I have chosen you to do the sacrifice," the Raja told him, expecting him to be honoured.

"But...but..." Madan began, only to be silenced.

"I know what you are going to say. There are many who are senior to you, and they should be given the opportunity, after Narayan passed away. But, I have

---

[8] Sculptor of the idol.

[9] The buffalo asura/demon in Hinduism.

made the selection. In you, I see the purity and faith I would like in the person who performs this all-important task."

And so the decision had been made, and Madan's fate sealed.

He had come home feeling low and depressed. For as long as he could remember, he had always managed to make himself scarce when the allotted time for the sacrifice arrived. Amid the frenzied beat of the *dhak,* and the choral blowing of conch shells, the bleating of the baby goat was drowned, but Madan heard it loud and clear, to the exclusion of anything else. It echoed inside him long after the act.

Sometimes, when the Devi was by herself, late at night, he would sit in front of her and ask, "Ma, do you really support and want this offering? The bloodshed, violence, and the screaming of the goat, mars the peace and tranquillity of the puja. I know this has been a tradition but I can't accept that you, present here with your children, would want to witness this, and have the audience also be a part of it. Can you not give some indication about what you want?"

She looked at him with all her intensity, but never answered his question. It seemed so ironic that this time she had isolated him from among all her devotees, to perform what to him was the most dreaded task. After all, the Raja was only a vehicle of her wishes. Of this he was convinced.

"Be a man. Grow up, Madan." These words broke into his reverie as his friend came and sat next to him, slapping him on the back. "Think of all those who would love to be in your shoes, getting all this importance," he said.

"There are so many other ways of getting importance and serving the Devi. Why this, and why me?" Madan mumbled. He knew his refusal to do the job would ignite the proverbial rage of the Raja. The consequences would spell disaster for his family. He had no choice but to comply.

The goddess arrived in all her glory and took her place in the *thakur dalan*. Nature too sang her praises with the dancing white *kash*[10] stalks against the clear, blue sky of the month of October, painted with billowy clouds. Madan wanted to be happy, to enjoy these few days with Ma Durga but the *katari*[11] that he had been given to sharpen and prepare for the sacrifice seared his insides.

"Make sure it is only one stroke. That is the way it should be done. Otherwise it is a taint on the puja," some elders warned him.

The words weighed on him heavy and ominous.

Even on the night of *Ashtami*[12], he found a moment alone with the Devi and spoke to her. He was angry, scared, and desperate. "What is this test that you are putting me through? Are you testing my belief in you or my ability to do a difficult task? You do not need the

---

10 A variety of long grass.
11 Blade.
12 Eighth day of Durga puja.

slaying of a helpless animal, by someone insignificant like me, to prove your powers. But, if you truly need me to have faith in my belief in you, then you need to prove yourself to me. The ball is now in your court. Someone has said that there is a god only because we, the ordinary beings, are there to give you that elevated position. Without a devotee there is no god and without a god there is no devotee. We both need each other. I will not plead with you anymore."

Navami[13] arrived. The puja had been progressing smoothly, and the celebrations were in full swing.

Then came the designated time for the sacrifice. All the people gathered around. The *dhakis* beat the drums, gradually building up the crescendo, while the women in the family, in their cream *gorod*[14] saris with vermilion borders, put the conch shells to their lips, breathed deeply and blew. There was a hush, other than the resounding call of the choral blowing. The goat was being brought to the sacrificial altar to be anointed. The place had been made holy with sprinkled *Gangajal*[15]. The Raja, in all his finery, placed himself on the ornate chair and nodded for the proceedings to begin.

The goat, sensing that there was danger ahead, struggled to get free, only to be held even more firmly. Its inconsolable bleating added to the palpable tension. Madan held the *katari* and walked up. He stared at the Devi, almost as a challenge. Then he looked at his target, sucked in a sharp breath, to prepare himself. Once again

---

[13] Ninth day of Durga puja.

[14] Heavy silk.

[15] Water from the holy Ganges river.

the frightened cry of the goat rang in his ears. He was resolute. The job had to be done.

The priest was ready to anoint the goat. But, somewhere in the emotional charge of the moment, the rope loosened, and the goat made its escape.

A gasp went through the crowd. The puja had been flawed. The deity was annoyed. The sacrificial offering to her had been refused. The *Rajbari* would be doomed. A startled Madan looked up and his eyes searched the expression of the Devi. Her eyes smiled and she looked calm.

In the confusion that followed, with people chasing the goat, the petrified animal, in a bid to save itself, instinctively rushed to the Raja and jumped into his lap, pleading for a safe haven. Even the goat realised that it was the Raja who would make the final decision.

Madan felt a rush of relief. There was no remorse at not having completed his duty. The Devi had answered his prayers. His abiding faith in her had been reaffirmed.

To Madan's surprise, Raja Raj Bahadur, too, was not infuriated. He spent a few moments deep in thought, considering the events that had just occurred. The goat pressed its trembling body to him, scared and apprehensive. He took a decision and addressed the gathering, "This humble creature has asked for my *sharan*[16] and it shall have it. Such an occurrence is a divine signal. I have never witnessed anything like this. It is the

---

16 Asylum or protection.

wish of Ma Durga to do away with this practice and so it shall be. From today, we will only offer a large gourd as a symbolic sacrifice."

This ritual continues.

10

Sadhan Chatterjee

He was the quintessential patriarch. At ninety-three, he continued his rule of terror and compassion. Strange bedfellows but that was the way it was. Sitting on his easy chair in the lounge that led into the other rooms, he had a view of the coming-ins and going-outs. He monitored the timings of the milkman, the maids, the driver, the newspaperman, and all the family members. More accurate than any branded watch, Judge Sadhan Chatterjee's body clock had never failed him in all these decades.

He was my great-grandfather.

"*Bouma,* you are late for the market this morning. All the best fish pieces would have gone by now," he said, as the senior-most daughter-in-law hurried down the stairs. "Kali, your morning walk has extended well beyond the regular time. The *shingara*[1] and *jilipi*[2] break, over the cup of sweet tea, squarely negates the benefit of your morning walk," he chided his sixty-three-year-old eldest-born, as the man sheepishly walked up the stairs, hoping his father would not notice.

---

[1] Samosa.

[2] Jalebi.

Robi, his second-born, enjoyed his constitutional pegs at the club, especially over the weekends and would often get back well after midnight. Taking off his shoes, he would creep up the stairs in his socks. Most mornings, after his escapades, he was greeted with a 'knowing' observation, and on one particular occasion, he was told, "One of these days, don't be surprised to get back to an empty room. How long will Malati spend sleepless nights waiting for your whistle to open the front door?"

"This is the fourth time this month that the newspaper has arrived well after my morning tea. Your family has been delivering the papers for nearly thirty years now and I could set my watch by the thud on the verandah when it fell. Late hours on the TV and mobile at night stops you from waking up on schedule, isn't it? You better change your habit if you wish to retain the job," was the threatening reprimand meted out to young Paresh when he came to take the money for the newspapers.

To the maid he said, "Parboti, I have noticed that you have been leaving between four-thirty and five instead of seven in the evening for the past two weeks. Strangely enough, driver Nirmal is also taking off early under some pretext or the other. And, instead of eight, you are now coming at around nine-thirty. By the time you arrive, breakfast is over and the ladies have started the preparations for lunch. What is the problem? Mornings are very busy and that is the time when maximum help is required. If this becomes your routine, it is not acceptable."

Alongside this aspect of his nature, he was also incredibly sensitive to the voice of the weak. He had his ways of finding out about the families of the household help and would quietly support them when their family members needed money for medical treatment, or a child's tuition fees; when someone was getting married, and at times, simply surprise them with money for a family day out to the movies, or a visit to an entertainment park, or a good meal at a restaurant if a child had performed well at something or on someone's birthday.

Did the man never sleep? Was there nothing that escaped his eagle eye or agile mind? Chatterjee Babu, as he was known, was a legend in Manik Para, the area he lived in. The Chatterjee house was a landmark for any person visiting the area for the first time, with its ornate, wrought-iron gates in an intricate paisley design, the fountain in front of the building, spouting jets of water from the marble vases held by the water nymphs in playful poses, the stately double-storied mansion itself with a large portico, carved pillars, decorated façade in lattice work, and large French windows, all of which spoke the language of an era lost in the twenty-first century surroundings of glass and metal and faux wood and plastic cane furniture. The grounds were vast and sprawling with terraced lawns.

There was a time when there were large cages on the lawns, with exotic birds and even a bear and a huge aquarium with sea mimicked water and strange water creatures, which were a magnetic draw for visitors. I loved the pond that was cradled by the coconut grove on one side of the compound. It was my own private swimming pool where I would cool off from the steam of summer and race the fish that were startled by my jumping in.

Unable to communicate with its towering, concrete neighbours, this little world had somehow frozen time in its own confines, and its pulse beat to the music of a forgotten melody. "I cannot imagine how people live in these cramped spaces they call apartments. I've been told they are very costly but why would people who have the money choose to live in expensive slums is beyond me. That is what they are, congested slums with hundreds of people breathing down your back. You can't even snore in peace! The walls are so thin that people can listen in to private conversations if the volume is a little loud. You can't even speak the way you want in these so-called homes. No wonder there are so many people who need to go to strangers to just talk. And, there is hardly any space for the family to live together," surmised Sadhan Chatterjee dismissively, to a family friend who, unknown to Chatterjee, was planning on moving into a flat himself for the sake of convenience! But he was not about to confess this to his friend, Chatterjee Babu, when he was in this vitriolic mood.

It was strange how I, the youngest in the family, felt equally at ease outside and inside the gates of my home. I was all of ten and Baro Dadu and I spent many afternoons together. He had a memory and clarity of thought that I now realise was most unusual for a person his age. But for me, then, it was most natural to go to him for maths lessons. Over ginger biscuits dipped in tea, we would work together on maths problems, and Baro Dadu would somehow relate it to real life, and also quiz me with mental maths questions.

"So Dadubhai," he would say, "we have thirty-five mango trees in the orchard and each tree bears about four hundred and fifty fruits. We need to divide the fruits amongst all sixteen of us in the household—so how many mangoes do you think you will eat this summer?"

As I busied myself calculating the numbers, he would pore over a much-thumbed favourite book of detective stories, chuckling to himself. "The suspect thought he was too clever but he cannot escape detective Niranjan's penetrating gaze or his superfast deduction prowess. The biscuit crumb on his sleeve and that on the victim is identical, meaning that they were together, though the suspect was denying it all along. You know, Dadubhai, greed is like a pit. It becomes one's fall. In this case, the man's weakness for cranberry cookies was the giveaway. Imagine! A measly crumble of a bit of biscuit to seal your fate." Little did I realise that this was my baptism into the art of writing detective novels, which is my passion and profession as an adult today. And then he would narrate interesting and tricky cases that he had to give his judgment on, in the process giving me insights into human behaviour that no textbook could ever teach me.

Occasionally, we would go to the market together, and he would take me to some of the eateries that had been there since his youth. "I am very bored with all the healthy food I am served at home. Light fish curry that looks like pond water, steamed vegetables that stare at me waiting to be fried, and dal that can go for a swim being so watery! The time has come for our rendezvous," he would whisper enticingly into my ears. Prawn thermidor and almond soufflé were his weaknesses and we would keep it a secret between us since he had been advised to lay off certain foods.

I didn't mind being his partner in crime, as I gorged on the delicacies! It was he who introduced me to the rich baked cheese samosas, flaky chicken patties with layers of crispy flour soaked in fat, subtle spring onion biscuits, stick jaw toffees that were a healthy challenge to a bull dog's so-called lock jaw, rich luscious dollops of almond drops, chocolate fudge oozing yumminess, and the unique drink of sweet thick *chafi* (mixture of tea and coffee with milk and jaggery).

In fact, mealtimes were unique experiences even at home. As the patriarch of the house he would be served his meal in a large bell metal plate with numerous small bowls surrounding it, each containing some unique item. It was always an elaborate Bengali meal following the sequential order of ghee with rice, followed by some bitter item, followed by vegetable dishes culminating in at least two fish preparations, then sweet chutney, papad, and a sweet dish. As he navigated through his meal, the various daughters-in-law would stand in attendance.

On one occasion, a fairly new bride was visiting and she was allowed the privilege of sitting next to him as he ate his meal solemnly. Baro Dadu followed a rather special ritual at the end of the meal. He had a penchant for cats of which there were at least ten, and they would partake of a bowl of milk and rice that was kept next to his food. On the floor, next to the table, ten bowls were laid out, and he would make a whistling sound once he finished eating. All the cats that had been waiting patiently under the large, round wooden table, would rush out and stand in front of their bowls, and he would pour the food out for them. It was quite a spectacle to one uninitiated in the ceremony. And it was quite a ceremony! So, as was his habit, that day, too, he finished his meal and made his unique whistling sound. In a flash, the felines jumped out from under the table, where they were waiting in the shadows. The new bride, unknown to the rest of the family, had a mortal fear of cats. I still remember the episode as clearly as if it had happened today. As the cats whizzed out, a few of them brushed past her sari and one managed to get entangled in the pleats of her sari. The poor lady let out a petrified scream and, all niceties forgotten, jumped up on the chair, and then leapt on to the table and unable to keep balance, fell into the patriarch's lap in a heap. There was a unanimous gasp from all the spectators as my poor Baro Dadu feebly tried to disentangle the bundle on his lap!

"Notun bou[3], now we all know your Achilles' heel. All we need to do is set a few cats free and voila! We can get you to do whatever we wish. Your dramatic reaction also alarmed these poor creatures into guzzling the food in a terrible hurry. We have to think of a way of befriending you with them to avoid future calamities," he teased her with a twinkle in his eye.

His eating escapades in restaurants were not the only secrets that had to be buried. Chatterjee Babu had been a renowned lawyer before taking on judgeship, and his ability to win even apparently hopeless cases was a subject of local lore. One particular case had been kept locked in the inaccessible vaults of the Chatterjee mind-drome. Like Voldemort, it was a subject that could not be named, let alone discussed. It happened many years

---

[3] New bride.

ago, and the story was narrated to me when I was much older, in hushed tones, lest even the walls repeat the incident.

"Today I will reveal a deadly secret to you since the same blood runs in your veins. Volatility, excitability, and unpredictability are some of its markers. We've been initiated into this circle of information purely for self-protection. Forewarned is forearmed, it is said. It is a caution to keep our bile in check. Too much of it makes us vulnerable to uncontrolled anger, resentment, jealousy, and envy," said my cousin one evening when we were by ourselves on the terrace. It was apparent that this was serious business and I listened with my whole body.

As with most large joint families, the Chatterjees, too, had many youngsters of similar ages. Baro Dadu's youngest nephew had been married to a beautiful lady of many talents. Her entry had set in motion a host of racing pulses within the family and many wished to curry favour with her. One of them was Baro Dadu's youngest son, who was close in age to his cousin, the husband of the lady. The young husband was completely besotted with his lovely wife but there was a medical problem. This was known to his parents but the wishful thinking was that everything would get sorted out once he got married. This had been conveyed to the son so convincingly that it had got embedded in his psyche. The idea that there was a sexual issue that needed to be dealt with was considered repellent. As the months rolled by, the new, young bride grew more distant from her husband who refused to consult a doctor for fear of being socially ridiculed.

"I would like to have a child. We cannot continue like this pretending that everything is all right. We need to visit a doctor. We could go to someone not known to others in the family," she had pleaded with him.

"The matter is all in your head, a figment of your imagination. You simply crave for attention from other men and try to put me down, to belittle and blame me. By making a public spectacle of me you are trying to prove your innocence and take the focus away from your inability to conceive. You are using your looks to humiliate me as not being good enough for you so that you can seek pleasure elsewhere. Your vanity disgusts me," lashed out the husband in a fit of rage, trying to project his guilt and shame on to her by blaming her. That became his shield in the mind war raging inside him, by denying the harsh reality that he knew existed.

His wife had no dearth of other suitors, and it was rumoured that Baro Dadu's son got cosy with her. She responded to his advances, hesitantly at first and then more willingly when she realised that she could not make any headway with her husband. When the matter became a little more apparent, the husband grew consumed with anger and jealousy. On one fateful night, he pulled the trigger on his cousin and shot him dead. The incident stunned the family into complete shock.

Other than the terrible loss, the matter was also one of family honour and name. Baro Dadu, the head of the family, took the reins even in that moment of deep loss and grief. He called his nephew aside, and advised him that if he wished to save himself from being charged with murder, put into prison or perhaps even hanged, it was imperative that he pretend he was insane. Not being of sound mind was his only path to saving himself. And that is exactly what happened. A young life had been snuffed out in a moment of uncontrolled anger, the lawyer had lost his child but he had saved and protected the family name. The nephew was moved to a mental asylum, and spent a few years there until he was declared mentally stable enough to return to his family. Needless to say, the secret stayed sealed within the family. And, while he was away, Baro Dadu procured a divorce for the young wife since her husband was not of sane mind, so that she was free to make a life for herself. I was told that a few years later she got married again to a man of her choice and did etch out a new life for herself.

There was yet another side to Baro Dadu that was most endearing. The house being large and rambling with people walking in and out, security was not of a particularly high order. With advancing age, Baro Dadu developed insomnia. He would wake up at odd hours and roam around the house until sleep befriended him. On one such late-night meandering, he found himself face-to-face with a burglar who had managed to creep into the house, waiting for a quiet time to complete his business. It is difficult to say who was the more surprised of the two. There was a scuffle, and Baro Dadu managed to push the man into the grilled room that contained the water pump and lock the door. Morning found Baro Dadu snoozing outside the grille with the thief inside. On waking up he asked the man, "What had you come to steal?"

"I am a pump mechanic and am good at stealing pumps. That is what I had come to take and then sell for a few hundred rupees," confessed the trapped thief.

By then the household was awake and a curious bunch of people stood around the pump room watching the proceedings. With the master of the house every altercation was like a hearing in the court! "The pump had been causing trouble and I am very relieved that you have the skills to fix it. Your punishment is that you will set this right and I will get the implements that you need. We have a tool shed with a whole array of instruments," declared the patriarch and asked for the implements to be brought.

The matter did not end there. Feeling sorry for the man being hungry (and perhaps feeling a trifle munchy himself), he called for the watchman to get some *kachoris*[4] and potato curry and tea to arm the newfound mechanic as he got busy! Not surprising that this thief turned pump technician became the regular person on call every time there was a pump problem! His loyalty to the master had been clinched.

It was said that Chatterjee Babu was a conservative man as far as religion was concerned. He would follow all the rituals expected of a Brahmin and eat rice cooked only by a Brahmin. These were the quirks in the man who otherwise had a generous view of the world. Inter-caste marriages within the family were taboo until the inevitable happened. One of the young men fell in love with a Muslim girl and was determined to marry her. No one in the family could broach the topic fearing an outburst. However, the young man was equally adamant. He would marry none other. The young girl

---

[4] Deep fried, stuffed bread.

visited the house and even met Baro Dadu but no one had spelt it out to him. Tension mounted. The old man was anything but a fool. He not only sensed the tension but also understood clearly that his permission would solve the impasse.

"Baro Dadu, tell me the story once again about my parents. I would not be here and we would not have our food escapades if you had not changed. What happened?" I urged him one afternoon when we were sitting on the verandah and he was teaching me the tricks of chess. Looking a little embarrassed and with a hint of a smile he said, "Dadubhai, your parents are very determined people and you are like them! I admit I was narrow-minded and rigid and your parents forced me to think differently. To tell you the truth, it is a big relief for me. Now we can go and eat anywhere and I don't have to worry about who is cooking the pilau! Actually, I liked Sanaa right from the start. She seemed to be a sensible and sensitive girl with a mind of her own. She did not push herself either but allowed me to take my time. I struggled with the situation within myself. It was years of belief that I had to shed, and that seemed like a Herculean task, but I had to take the call for the peace of the family and for myself. So, one day when she was visiting, I called her and requested her to cook biryani. I told her that I had not tasted authentic home-made biryani in a long time and I had heard that their family had a special recipe. You should have seen everyone's expression. They couldn't believe what they were hearing. The sigh of relief all around echoed in a chorus across the entire building! And I must say your mother did a terrific job with the biryani and the kebabs. And, at the end of it all, I got you. A winner all through. What do you say?" I couldn't agree more. I couldn't have asked for a happier childhood.

11

Snake Family

I had heard of people who kept snakes as pets. I had never met someone who actually cuddled snakes! So, when our house help, Shankar, told me the story, I was intrigued.

Before joining us in Siliguri, he had been a farmer, living in his village in Odisha. One day, while harvesting the dry crop, he accidently hacked a mother cobra that had a few babies with her. Shankar has always been close to the soil, and even in his more urban avatar, does not think twice about rescuing squirrels, birds, and even civet cats. So, the guilt of orphaning the snake babies weighed heavily on him. He brought home one baby.

"Even as a baby it could put up its hood and look beautiful and dangerous at the same time," he declared, proudly. To ensure that the snake remained harmless to him and the humans around, he defanged it, with professional help from a snake charmer, who told him exactly what he needed to do to keep it that way.

"And what did you do with it?" I asked, curious to know the details of their relationship.

"Oh! We became good friends," he answered casually, adding that people in the village would all call him '*Shib Thakur*'[1].

"And why so?" I enquired.

"It would travel with me wherever I went, and found it comfortable to coil itself around my neck and shoulders. Occasionally, it would sit with its hood up. It grew to be a big snake and had a beautiful hood," he reminisced, fondly.

"Weren't the people scared?" I asked, my own fears overcoming me.

"No, they knew I made sure that it had no poison. I gave it its own bed. It was a big covered basket, and it would slip into it and fall asleep."

"And what did you feed it?" My questions simply kept popping out.

"I gave it eggs, and sometimes it even tasted the food I ate, though I don't think it appreciated it much. Once it became big, it would even go out on its own, probably hunt a bit, and then come back. But it needed to go out. We all need freedom, don't you agree? Only one day I got a bit scared."

"Really, you were scared? That must have been something weird, to frighten you. What was it?" I was all ears.

"One afternoon, I came home from work and heard some noises coming from the basket. I lifted the cover and what I found..." He left the sentence unfinished.

---

[1] Lord Shiva, the Hindu god who is depicted with a snake around his neck.

"Well, go on," I said.

"Well," he smiled, prolonging the moment, "I found three cobras in the basket!"

"What! How did that happen?"

"Oh. Don't you understand? It went out on its own, as I had mentioned, and it must have talked about its safe home with the other snakes. I think they wanted to feel safe, too, and be sure of getting food. Besides, he must have been lonely and wanted a partner. It is just that two others decided to join him. After all, I could only partially fulfil his need for companionship. I could not speak his language, and he needed to speak freely, and have others around him who understood him," explained Shankar, with rare compassion and understanding.

"And then?" I asked, holding my breath and feeling a little foolish at not being able to understand the most natural and simple things in life, like wanting a family, needing friends, and inviting them to one's home, perhaps for a drink."

"And then I got a person who catches snakes to defang the other two. Being a professional, he knew exactly what to do and visited us on a regular basis. We lived happily together! But..."

"So there is a 'but' after this happy ending? What happened?" I asked, my curiosity piqued again.

"Life's journey has no ending until there is an end to life. It is not like a movie with 'The End' written on the last frame," said a philosophical Shankar. "Things were going on comfortably, though some people in the village looked at me strangely and felt that I was queer in the head. One senior even suggested getting a local shaman to carry out some rites on me to rid me of my madness. They were convinced that I was possessed by some evil snake demon."

"How did you handle this pressure? It must have been quite traumatic. Since you had reared the snake from infancy, you were obviously attached to it. But, do snakes show affection in any way? How did you know it was attached to you?"

"Any living creature has a heart. It has feelings. You don't need to be a doctor or a scientist to understand this. Even a plant looks happy when you greet it and water it. And, it shrinks if you curse it. These creatures don't think so much or look for meanings in every action. They simply are. And, if you let them be, they let you be. It is humans who complicate matters. In my case, too, the inevitable happened. I got married."

"And things got complicated, is it?"

"You could say so. Bina, my wife, knew about the snakes since she is from a village close to mine, but she had not really thought about what it would be like to live with a snake family. I had met her occasionally and found her attractive. I was earning well, had no major addictions other than the occasional drink that I had with my friends, and did not have any encumbrances that my wife would be saddled with. So, you could say that I was a good candidate for husband material. And her parents agreed to the proposal since I had a soft corner for her."

"So, you got the wife you wanted. The snake family had settled into a routine. How did complications crop up?"

"Bina had to stay in the same room as the snakes because that was my bedroom. Knowing about the snakes, as I soon realised, was one thing, but when she had to share actual space with them, it was a different matter altogether. She could not sleep at night in the fear that they would climb on to the bed and if she did manage to doze off for a while, she would wake up screaming with nightmares."

"So, are you saying that it reached a point where it was a choice for you between your wife and the snakes?"

Trying to imagine the scenario was bizarre but amusing for me at the same time, though I must admit that secretly my sympathies were entirely with Bina. Recreating the scene mentally where I would have to cohabit with hisses and slithers and darting of long forked tongues and shed snake skins, however harmless, gave me scales all over. But, of course, I could not disclose my leanings in any way, knowing how sensitive Shankar was about the matter. I was interested in the story and had to keep a straight face, and occasionally empathise with his predicament, however false it was! The fact that I was not doing a good job of it soon became apparent.

"You are making fun of me, heart of hearts, aren't you? They were like my babies, you have to understand that. I had Bina's parents and other village elders coming over to visit me and they advised me to get rid of the snakes. In the meanwhile, Bina had gone off to stay with her parents. She refused to come back until she felt safe. Besides, she was pregnant and being in the comfort of her parents' home was important. I had tried to reason with her about the harmlessness of the snakes, considering the fact that they had done nothing to her, but no logic worked."

"So, you were compelled to get rid of them. Yes, you are right. I can understand better what Bina was experiencing, though I can also sense your pain. What did you do?"

"I did the only thing I could. I took them all out and placed them far away from my home. I also carried their baskets so that they would not be completely homeless. Can you place yourself in their position? To wake up one morning and suddenly find you have been abandoned? I had to ensure that my doors were sealed so that they would not make their way back. It was heartbreaking for me. But, I was not heartless and irresponsible. Every day I made sure that I would carry some food for them because they were used to getting it. It was a blessing that they used to go out on their own even when living with me, so the outdoors was not alien to them.

I actually believed that I was sinning for the second time, the first time being the accident when I killed the mother. My repentance was giving that baby a home and now I was snatching it away. It might sound absurd and melodramatic to you but I was convinced that I would be cursed by the snake goddess who we worship in my tribe."

This was getting complex with many more layers being added to the story. Religious beliefs, guilt, fear, affection, social pressure, anger, frustration, and a motley of other ingredients were getting churned and creating explosive material inside Shankar, looking for a vent to explode. Admirably, he managed to contain it, and divert it by becoming a volunteer with the forest officials, and reporting poaching of animals or cutting of trees in the wooded areas close to his home. This did not win him popularity amongst the villagers but it did give him some peace.

With nature taking its course, his wife gave birth to a little boy and she came back to live with Shankar. The initial tensions having got eased out, they both got engrossed in their progeny. Shankar, being good with his hands, made a cradle with bamboo and jute for his child and the baby spent many happy hours swinging in it. Bina would do the housework and occasionally give the cradle a gentle push to let her baby know that he was not alone.

The temperature started falling with the onset of winter. As was the practice in the village, Bina would massage her child with mustard oil and then put him out in the winter sun, to soak in the goodness of sunlight and build strong bones. She would do this every day and keep him in the cradle in front of her hut, for an hour or so, and check up on him, in between her chores.

It was another regular day and the baby was sunbathing and Bina was cooking inside the house. Shankar was working in the field. There was a sudden disturbance with loud noises that made Bina rush outside. The sight chilled her to the bones. A small leopard, known to carry away little babies, was leaning over the cradle and around its legs was entangled a large cobra! The two wild animals were engaged in a desperate fight. The leopard had obviously just made its appearance when the cobra stepped into the scene. The feline was determined to snatch the baby and the cobra was set on not allowing that to happen.

"I was coming back from the field when some villagers came running to tell me that my baby was in danger. The commotion had attracted the neighbours living close to my house and they had gathered around. I ran as fast as I could and arrived to find that people were using stones and long sturdy sticks to frighten away the leopard. My child was crying so much that he was getting choked and finding it difficult to breathe. The cobra had wrapped itself around the back of the leopard and was hanging on. The leopard, furious to have got distracted and lost its prey, was attacking the snake with its teeth. I don't know if the cobra could have handled the leopard on its own but it certainly bought us time to step in and do the needful.

The presence of so many people, the stones and sticks, and the hands-on combat with the cobra, finally made the leopard turn around and slink away, into the forest. Bina had rushed to the baby and was trying to soothe him. I ran to her side and together we caressed our child and took him to the health centre for a check-up.

But before going, I went up to my first child, my cobra, that had saved my son. It was obvious that though we had moved him out of the house, he lived in the vicinity, and kept vigil on us. He must have noticed the predator and realised the danger and swiftly moved into action, risking his own life. Bina, who had been so terrified, wept tears of gratitude. And, from the next day onwards, it was she who took the eggs for the cobras to eat and left them in a place where they would come for it!

The village elders agonised over the matter. Having been witness to the proceedings they could not simply write me off as a peculiar specimen of humankind who had strange obsessions. At the same time, they had to justify their previous stand against the reptiles. The senior-most came up with his own theory and deductions, and the others nodded their heads, sagely, in agreement. 'Actually, I can now see the picture clearly. Shankar and the cobra have a past life connection and they both need to pay off their debts to each other. So, what we are seeing now is a form of cosmic play, far beyond our mundane human comprehension.'

I listened quietly to all this discourse and did not get into any debate. As I have mentioned earlier, I don't believe in thinking or analysing too much, like my animal friends. I was just happy that they would now let us be and I would let my animal friends be, content in the knowledge that we share a rare bond."

12

Stopgap Hero

"Learn from him. His attitude is so commendable. The epitome of team spirit." The words rang loud and clear and he could hear the applause beating against his eardrums. It hurt. Even today. Even after thirty-five years. He was fifty years old.

The grand hall of the Calcutta Youth Academy was packed as it usually was during the morning assembly. The drama teacher was delivering an 'inspirational' speech. It was his turn that morning to help build men of substance. He had chosen Sagar as the case study for the validation of his message. "Look beyond yourself. Think of the greater good."

And the reason why Sagar was held up as the shining star? The incident. It was an interschool play competition. A prestigious one. A chance to shine on stage, unearth the latent histrionic talent festering inside. Festering because it had been languishing unrecognised for too long and needed acknowledgement. Better still it needed generous doses of praise to nurse its deflated ego.

And, of course, with it came the opportunity to impress the female population that was floating around. He could do with some recognition from them. It would be fodder for his self-esteem, which had been deprived of nutrition for a while.

Sagar was to play the unscrupulous village money lender. There was also the local land shark, the promoter, a slithery character who manipulated the villagers into selling their land for a sniff of money. Practice began in full swing. Sagar poured his heart into the role. He also invested his hopes, dreams, and ambitions into depicting the crafty manoeuvrings of the man, in front of the mirror, to try and better his own performance.

"Sagar, think of your studies. Acting is not your future. That will not earn you your bread and butter," cautioned his concerned parents, but Sagar was oblivious to these minor issues. He was en route to stardom!

A couple of days before the final show, the organiser had arranged a dress rehearsal for setting the lights, music, and other technical requirements. Sagar's school came up on stage and enacted the play. It was a sort of a mock test and the actors were all charged up. The small audience consisting of the other school participants and the managers were spellbound. However, soon after they came off-stage, the grave-faced organiser came up to the drama teacher and said, "We really enjoyed your production, and you stand a very good chance of winning, but you have one extra member. We had specified eight characters at most, and you have nine. Either you bring it down to eight or we will have to disqualify you."

The cast was in shock. The drama teacher faced a deep dilemma. What was he to do?

There was a meeting of the entire cast, to discuss this sensitive and delicate issue. Suggestions trickled in about how the script could be tightened to reduce the number of characters. To cut the tedious and painful process short, Sagar found he was getting cornered into accepting that the play could be done with the land shark doubling as the moneylender. Sagar was the only one who was dispensable.

"What can I say?" remarked the teacher. "It has to be a team decision. After all, we are all trying to keep the school flag flying high."

Though the intense disappointment drained the life from him, Sagar was compelled to accept the verdict and not create a scene. The teacher said, "Sagar's maturity and commitment to the needs of the school must be applauded. We all need to learn from him."

Sagar's heart was breaking. Every cell in his body was screaming out against this injustice. He did not feel mature or great at all. He was merely a lamb who had been slaughtered for a cause and then held up as a shining example to suit other people's needs and rectify someone else's mistake. He did not want to step down, but the praise from his teacher and the pats from his teammates trapped him in the heroic image he felt suffocated by, a hero who would be forgotten the moment the show was over. He was just a stop-gap hero who would be remembered as the 'poor fellow who had to face an unfortunate situation'. And the real heroes would be those who would get the applause, praise, media coverage, and the *oohs* and *aahs* from the girls. They would also get the certificates and the chance to write on their CVs that they were members of the award-winning play.

Their play did win and receive rave reviews, which Sagar read, almost like a masochistic exercise. Nowhere was his name mentioned, not even in the school magazine, as the boy whose sacrifice had made it possible for the play to be staged.

And so the years had gone by. Sagar had plastered his broken heart with bandages of "there'll always be a next time; it is all a part of growing up and becoming a complete man; it is these disappointments that strengthen the mettle". There never came the second chance to be on stage.

At home, too, he was always the elder brother who had to be responsible and 'generous'. His younger brother had arrived nearly ten years after him, and was the little darling whose every wish was their parents' command. "Give him that mango, Sagar, you can always have one later. After all, he will learn from your example if you share your portion. He needs to have a hero in you he can follow," his mother would say. There were many such incidents where he had to play the role model for the 'impressionable younger sibling'.

"He needs to grow up too. When will he learn to adjust? He will be looking to see who the hero will be when the situation demands, instead of being one himself. He is too used to having his own way all the time," protested Sagar. His brother was five and was insisting on playing a video game on television when Sagar was watching a science fiction serial. His parents, choosing quiet in the house instead of taking on a five year old throwing a tantrum, pleaded with Sagar to watch the replay of the serial at a later time.

"You are older and more mature. He will learn with time," said his mother, justifying her stance.

"Was I ever allowed these allowances? I was expected to be the noble one, who always had to think of the greater good if anyone needed to step back. The supposed goodness in me has become my biggest challenge, my greatest obstacle in my personal journey. I am fed up with being the *bhalo chele*[1]," lashed out Sagar.

But despite all this internal friction, life went on. He was a diligent student, secured good grades in school and college, got himself a stable job and a demure life companion, and they had two children. There had been no further major incidents where he had to suffer the inner faceoff between being adjusting or choosing to disregard the greater good for personal benefit.

However, as a parent, the one thing that he did ensure was never to impose on his daughter and son the 'being good' quotient. Once old enough to appreciate his advice, he told them, "You don't need to be a crab and bring others down to pursue your own goal, but at the same time, don't give up on your dreams just to accommodate other people all the time. Don't live with regrets. Do something for others even if it means compromising on your own ambition, only if it brings you joy and your heart is with you. It is a no-win situation if you get taken for granted."

"Baba, have you ever been taken for granted?" asked his daughter, sensing her father's liquid upheaval inside him.

---

[1] Good boy.

"Where do you think all this advice is coming from?" he replied, and left it at that.

Sagar's unfulfilled desire to win fame and public recognition remained, until an opportunity did come his way, at work. It was a joint-venture project with a foreign delegation and Sagar was the most qualified for the job. He became the key person who worked with the team, to draw up the blue prints and plan future progression.

It soon became apparent that the Indian company needed to have a representative based in New York, and Sagar was the obvious contender for the post. He was thrilled. It was a dream opportunity to live in the most happening city and be a part of the web that would build the future. Finally, he was to get his place under the sun, and the recognition he so thoroughly deserved.

When the papers were being finalised, the dragon raised its head, the phantom dragon whose purpose it seemed was to rob Sagar of his moments of reckoning. Processing visa papers was taking time, and the post needed to be filled in a hurry. The company decided to recruit someone locally in New York.

Sagar could feel the old hollow sensation taking over. It was a sinking feeling. He wanted to scream out and say, "Just give it a little more time. The papers will get done. What is this enormous hurry? I deserve this post. I have worked for it."

Once again, he heard the politically apt words from his boss at work, "I'm so sorry. We all recognise you have nursed this project from its inception. You are integral to the company and we know you will always have its best interests at heart. Your guidance to the new recruit from here will be invaluable."

Once again, Sagar was portrayed as the selfless man who was ever understanding, pushing his interests to the rear, for the greater good. He was livid and frustrated with being a 'framed hero', trapped in the gilded, ornate package of the good man.

He had just reached the age of fifty. Life had slowly limped back to a kind of normalcy. However difficult it was for him to accept the situation, he had no option but to swallow his acute disappointment, though the bitter reflux did trouble him now and then. New matters were coming up, and the double-storied family house was now the issue. His parents had passed away, and the two brothers had to divide the property.

The first-floor flat had six rooms, while the ground floor had four. According to the will, Sagar was given the top floor flat, while the younger brother had the ground floor and some extra cash and gold.

The brother had three children, while Sagar had two. Used to always having his way and sure that the older brother would continue to play the role of the ever-accommodating individual, the brother declared, "You don't need that much space. I am sure you understand this. I have three children, so I will take the flat upstairs and compensate you with some money. We just need to decide how much."

Something rebelled inside Sagar and the *bhalo chele* role model snapped violently. His wife had always dreamed of living on the first floor and had planned her patch of green on the balcony where they would enjoy their morning tea, while looking at the wide, verdant expanse of the South Kolkata park in front, and watch the little children laugh and play. He had mentally designed one room as his study and music room, where he would relax and sketch. Drawing and painting was a hobby he never had the time to pursue, and retirement was the freedom he was waiting for, to pick up his easel again. His children too had longed for a den of their own which they would now finally have. He was not going to allow anyone to ride over him and crush his aspirations and those of his own family.

"No," he said, "It does not suit me. I want the first floor flat. I have my plans and I cannot accept your proposition, however convenient it may be for you."

The brother was astounded. He had assumed the family hero would quietly accept the proposal and adapt to the situation. Who was this alien Sagar who had found a voice and spread his wings to soar and claim his bit of the sky, the sun, the moon, and his bite of life as his own?

That evening when the brother's disgruntled family assembled for dinner to discuss the matter and rethink their future plans, since Sagar had spoken his mind, there was an agitated outpouring from the brother. "This is unthinkable. What has come over him? He is now the senior most in the family and should look out for all of us. We need the space much more than him. Besides, the flat upstairs has a better view and he should be generous enough to give it to us. We have always looked up to him as our role model. How selfish can he be!"

Sagar and his family too discussed the matter over dinner. His children had been witness to the altercation between the two brothers. His demure wife, who had been a quiet support all the years, said, "Your father will sleep peacefully tonight. He stood up for himself and for us, for what is rightfully ours."

"You have not allowed others to take you for granted," added his daughter.

"And Baba, now you will not live with any regrets, right?" said his son.

Sagar smiled. He felt validated and applauded. By himself and by those who mattered most to him. He had been a role model once again, only this time he had not compromised on his dreams.

13

The Conch

The golden sand was warm and soft under my bare feet. The sunbeams were trapped in the porous grains, and with each squelchy step, the solar power charged my tired muscles a little more. It was just about sunset. I had walked far away from the crowded part of the beach. The vendors with sweet, piping-hot masala lemon tea, the young boys with bottles of pungent massage oil, ready to knead the neck and feet with promises of instant relief from creaky painful joints, the men selling 'genuine pearls' and shell wares, and those offering small spicy samosas in paper packets, did not find it profitable to populate the fringes of the sea on this part of the beach.

In my solitude, I was contemplating the most recent events in my life. Sleep had forsaken me in the last month and fatigue of mind and body had become my constant companions. I was deeply exhausted and tired of trying to keep my business afloat, worn out looking after my ailing aunt who had brought me up, and fed up with keeping the spark alive in my romantic involvement. It was always me who seemed to be making all the adjustments to keep us together.

Unprecedented fiscal developments had taken the wind out of global trade and my export garments had piled up in warehouses. Trisha, my love interest, was finding her research in high-altitude mammals more interesting than me. My aunt, who had retired after a long stint in the education department, was suffering from ailments related to a lack of something productive to do with her life and was in depression. In short, I was feeling down and out and rather sorry for myself, and was not particularly scintillating company.

"Release your worries in a bubble into the universe and let it take care of them. You just chill," my childhood friend, Rajan, had sagely advised me after a couple of chilled beers one balmy night.

"Bah! All hogwash," I had snapped back. "Keep all your philosophical mumbo jumbo to yourself, and solve your own tangles. Blow a bubble indeed! It is the universe itself that is turning against me. Every single damn planet is casting its shadow on my happiness from every angle. 'Align your mind and body to the vibrations around you,' is what that smooth-tongued inspirational speaker said, the one whose talk you and I attended. Those very vibrations are twisting my world into a sailor's knot, which is impossible to undo. There is no escape from this vortex."

"It is interesting that you should use the word vortex. I am convinced it is your subconscious speaking. Have you not heard of a spiritual vortex?"

"Don't toodle off into another one of your fanciful theories. I have no patience for that, definitely not now. You just have a penchant for bringing in the surreal into all conversation. Let's just walk on terra firma for once and look at what is actually visible. And, what is clearly evident in my life right now is rumbling, dark, ominous clouds. I can hear them, see them, feel them."

"Whatever you may be seeing and feeling, there is a school of thought which believes vortexes are spiritual super-centres. Positive energy vortex sites, according to this theory, include the Giza pyramids, Stonehenge, and the Incas in Peru, among many others. These spiritual vortexes are believed to be cross-points between energy fields in the Earth's grid system.

In some areas, where these lines intersect, there is a concentration of energy, resulting in psychic enhancement and spiritual healing. Like a magnet, a spiritual vortex can align different parts of our spiritual make up to create a balance in our body. There have also been suggestions that vortexes can act like portals into other realms. And, who knows, in your case it could mean astral travel taking you to peaceful spiritual dimensions, where your problems will be minimised.

Why not think of your vortex as a magical place, a point of entry into a space where the bits of the jigsaw puzzle in you will feel aligned? Did you know that the seven *chakras* in our own bodies are said to be mini personal vortexes, energy-focuses, that power our life force? You really need something, anything, to make you receptive to these powers."

"You have succeeded in confusing the hell out of me and whatever clarity I might have had is now definitely lost forever. I feel like I am a walking, talking criss-cross of lines, to be more precise, 'energy lines' about to go kaboom! And, to add to the explosion, there is the fear of wandering off into another world, where I won't even have you to let off steam. Do me a favour. Let me just be and stew in my misery. It is better than becoming vapour, mist or a lightning conductor in some energy field!"

Rajan smiled a benign smile. "You are in one of your moods. Nothing will penetrate your personal Lennon wall."

"Are you referring to the John Lennon Wall in Prague? These geographical meanderings and ambiguous references to obscure walls (okay not quite unknown) is making me dizzy, bro. I get your concern to help me find love, peace, and freedom, like the writings on the wall, but you need to give me something more than mere theory and poetical illusions."

"I have left my graffiti on your wall for whatever it is worth. Have a look when you are calmer. Find the catalyst for change."

Having given me this dose of free and unsolicited *gyan*[1], he left me to my devices.

The last of the fading sun's rays glistened on the shimmering water and appeared to caress something that lay on the mute sand. Hastening my steps, I walked up to it, eager to investigate. It was an opaque, pristine, white shell, a conch actually, perfect in shape and dignified in its demeanour. Yes, that was the word—dignified, and elegant. It was not too large, just six inches in length and four inches in breadth, and yet its presence was commanding. I was close to it by now and wondered whether to pick it up when the impending crash of a large wave made the decision for me. It was clear that

---

[1] Advice.

the wave would drag the shell away with it. I knew I needed to pick it up before that happened.

Nestling it in my palms, I examined it. There was no creature inside. Gingerly, I put the open end to my ear in anticipation. Even as a child, this had always intrigued me and once again I was not disappointed. In its fragile being, the shell seemed to carry the raging water and the mysteries of the boundless ocean. I could hear the churning waves, and the wonder of it all left me at a loss for words. Somewhere from deep within me came a response.

By now, the moon was riding the heavens, and I turned around, heading back to the hotel with my gift from the depths of the mighty water. Mystic Waves was, providentially, the name of the hotel and I decided to have an early dinner at the restaurant before retiring to my room. Placing the conch carefully on the table, I was studying the menu when a gentleman came up to me.

"Hello, sir," he said, looking at the conch with evident excitement. "Where did you get this?"

"On the beach," I replied and enquired, "Why do you ask?"

Unable to contain his curiosity and agitation he responded, "Really! I am amazed that you found such a treasure on the open beach. This is a unique piece. It is a perfect *'Dakshinavarti Shonkho'*. The opening is on the opposite side unlike common shells and there is an imprint of five fingers, which is most unusual."

All this left me confused, and I must admit, uneasy. "So, what does this all mean?" I asked, a little nervously.

"Oh! It means that you are a very lucky man, and a chosen one, to have been given this. Keep it carefully and guard it well. There will be many who will know its value and seek it if they know it is with you. Let me tell you that this will be a turning point in your life."

And with these words, the man said his goodbyes and left, leaving me on edge. What was I supposed to do or expect to happen?

Dinner neglected, my fingers automatically wrapped themselves around what was now an added worry in my life. I glanced surreptitiously around the dining hall, to see if anyone else was watching. Gulping down the food, I exited the restaurant and took refuge in the sanctity of my room after locking the door. Could I have no peace?

The next morning I made my way to the station to board a train for Kolkata, acutely aware of my status as the 'chosen one'. I guarded the shell fervently till I reached home.

My aunt seemed to be well up on the significance of my gift when I showed it to her. "Oh! I had seen a piece like this at a friend's house years ago. She would only show it to her trusted ones. Guard it carefully. You have been given a special responsibility."

"To hell with this responsibility," I muttered. This supposed charm was only bringing me anxiety. I simply put it away in my almirah and shut the door firmly. However, niggling hopes of a miracle continued to plague me. Something astounding would happen to wash all my troubles away and I would float around free and light. One evening, I opened the cupboard, took out the conch, stared at it for a while, and, with my eyes closed, urged it to show its mystical strength, to prove that it was not mere calcium carbonate.

Nothing extraordinary happened, and days slipped by as I got back to my routine.

But I did research the object that was supposed to harbour mystic powers. A *shankh* or conch, amongst Hindus, is sacred and is blown before the start of any important activity. It is chiefly of two kinds, based on the direction of its coiling. The *Vamavarti* is the commonly found variety that coils leftwards. The *Dakshinavarti* or *Lakshmi Shankh* is the shell of a large sea snail usually from the Indian Ocean. Its uniqueness is that when held with the spout pointed upwards, its spiral twists to the right, making it rare.

The right spiral is supposed to reflect the movement of the planets. It is believed to nullify the negative effects of the planets in the life of the worshipper. I was convinced that in my horoscope, the planetary positions, at that point in time, were all messed up.

It is also believed to be the home of the Hindu goddess of wealth, Lakshmi, the consort of Lord Vishnu. Mentioned in the ancient Hindu scriptures, this conch is supposed to protect the devotee and bring peace, prosperity, good health, knowledge, and also give a boost to new business ventures. Devotee or not, I certainly needed Lakshmi to place her palms on my turbulence within, and restore peace and prosperity in my life.

This special conch is said to have an important place in Buddhist beliefs. The hair whorls on Buddha's head spirals to the right and the swirl of his navel, resembles this conch. Some say it helps to arouse the disciples from the slumber of ignorance and move towards a path of self-development and greater good. I was more than willing to be awakened from my stupor but who was going to make that call?

Somewhere in my readings I had also come across a reference that the *Dakshinavarti Shankh*, according to an old text, has the power to defeat the enemy of the devotee. Who were my enemies? How would I spot them? And how was the war going to be fought?

I pondered over all that I had read and I could see the graffiti on my Lennon wall with Rajan's words that said that I needed to look for the catalyst for change. I needed something to make me receptive to the mystical powers.

Over a month later, I met Rajan on the street. We were waiting to cross the road when he looked at me and exclaimed, "You look like a changed man! No creases, no frown or scowl, and a spring in your steps. Wow! What happened? Don't tell me you blew the bubble!"

The 'walk' light turned green, and I said playfully, "Actually, I did just that! Thanks for your counsel. You should follow your own advice, Rajan. It will help you get unentangled!"

His face was the picture of surprise as he struggled to find an answer. Meanwhile, I crossed the road feeling pleased with myself and my repartee.

Back home, I pondered over what he had said and peered at the mirror. It occurred to me that that for a few days I had slept soundly and woken up feeling like my earlier self, the one I seemed to have lost. It had happened quietly and seamlessly and I had not even noticed!

Had my troubles vanished? No. But they didn't seem oppressive anymore. So, what had changed? Had my life changed? Had I changed?

Yes, my life had changed. Picking up courage, I had finally called Trisha and discussed my feelings about our relationship and where it seemed to be headed. The fear of a negative response had kept me in limbo and I had been dangling like a goat about to be skinned. Surprised by the call, she seemed hesitant to make a commitment for the long term. "I don't know how long the research will take and it will require my presence here, in the mountains, till all the data gets collected."

Taking the cue, I immediately took the decision. "Yes, I can understand that but it is not possible for me either to wait indefinitely. We cannot carry on like this, so it is better to part ways now, when we are still friends." I said it with a firm finality but without any anger or bitterness. Strangely, voicing my response was uplifting. I was not sad or upset. Instead, there was relief and a sense of freedom, from my own anxiety and uncertainty.

Trisha's initial silence, over the phone, at my response, was telling. She obviously had not expected this, having got used to me making the compromises, in our five-year partnership. "Oh. I was not prepared for this. I thought we could go along the way we were for a couple of years more and then take a call. But, if this is your decision, I will have to accept it."

On the work front, the global market had shown marginal improvement but not enough to power the wind in my sails. To keep my ship afloat and visit fresh harbours, I had to make a few bold decisions. Instead of staying cocooned in the safety of garment exports, that had been the family business, I explored new pastures.

Knowledge and education would never go out of vogue. For as long as I could remember, I had dreams of being an educationist. I had never pursued it. There was a respectable ring to it and I hoped to contribute to the community. Yet, I had held back. Taking the risk gave me cold feet and all the possible disasters that could happen stared at me in the face.

It now seemed the right time to live the dream. I owned a plot of land that was lying vacant and I set the plans afoot to build the institution.

One evening, my astute aunt, who though ailing but ever observant, asked me, "So, finally, you are doing what you were meant to. Seeing you unhappy made me miserable too. Now I feel so much better. Let me know if I can be of some help. I still know some people who might be able to guide you."

I could hear a note of excitement in her voice after a long time.

And then she asked, "Where have you kept your special *shonkho*? I wanted to show it to my friend but did not know where it was."

The conch! I had almost forgotten about it, having kept it in the innards of my cupboard. Rushing to my room, I took out Nature's gift. So, what had it done for me? Were all the claims regarding its mysterious powers true after all? Was the arrival of the conch a turning point in my life?

The answers were not with me. But this much I did know. My enemy did not exist outside of me. There was no war that I needed to fight with any external force. I had become my own adversary. I had chosen to ignore the choices open to me.

Nothing had changed. Yet everything had. I had changed. And, I had the spirit of the mighty ocean next to me.

14

The Foot Doctor

I have to admit I ill-treated my feet. Relegating them to the less interesting, distant suburbs, my TLC (tender, love, and care) was focused on the more happening heart and head, where all the action was. Occasionally, I would get feelers of, "I also exist" but I disregarded them. After all, the foot would not contribute to my amateur attempts at scintillating conversation, and neither could it assist me in feeling the passionate recklessness of emotions. It was of no help to my intellectual or romantic pursuits.

Little did I realise its nuisance value to my esoteric ambitions. My feet had feelings and those had been injured. Its self-respect had been compromised by my deliberate dismissal of all attempts at seeking an appointment. Having done all the load bearing for all the years, being taken for granted, not complaining ever, it had had enough of being humiliated. Rebellion was a natural fallout. And, that did happen.

One morning, I realised I could not put my foot down. My big toe looked like an over-ripe pulsating tomato and a ginger-check of the soles, indicated that they could give a crocodile a run for its money. It was winter, the socks had camouflaged matters, but now there was an emergency at hand. I could no longer ignore my feet.

Besides, there was no way I could distract myself with cerebral and 'feeling' matters if nerve endings throbbed painfully.

Out came the contact list on the much thumbed phone and a call was put through to the foot magician, Mr Dutt.

"Hello, Mr Dutt. It's been a long while since we spoke. I need an appointment urgently. There is an in-growing toenail that needs immediate attention."

It needs to be explained that this gentleman has been an institution in Kolkata. Generations have benefitted from his services. He takes great umbrage if referred to as the person who does a pedicure. "I am a chiropodist. A gentleman was brought all the way from Canada, by the company I worked for, to train me. Would you go to a general doctor if you needed specific dental treatment? No, you would not. I have clients all over the world. They send me pictures of their feet to ask for my expert opinion about the course of action to follow." In short, he takes enormous pride in his expertise and you feel safe in his care.

"This week I'm totally booked. Next Monday?"

It was only Thursday and the wait till Monday seemed impossible, given the intensity of the rebellion by my feet. "I cannot wait that long in this condition. Please, give me some time tomorrow. Only you can be my saviour," I pleaded.

I could almost see the glow on his face. Promising him extra money or giving him one more client would cut no ice with him. Appealing to his pride in his skill was the only way. Give him a foot in desperate need and he would be the friend you are searching for. "There is a window tomorrow. After one visit I have a lunch appointment. I could visit you in-between but it would mean that I will be late for lunch."

"Oh, thank you very much. It is such a relief. I will keep your favourite lemon tea with a dash of rock-salt ready." I could hear the octogenarian chuckle softly.

Friday dawned with the promise of relief. Armed with a flask of lemon tea I welcomed Mr Dutt. Jauntily dressed in a bright T-shirt and denims, with a full head of dyed black hair, he exuded energy and a zest for life. A stickler for sanitisation, he took out an array of antiseptic lotions and creams, disposable blades and instruments. I had arranged for a bucket of hot water, towels and a low chair on which he sat, cradling my foot on his lap.

"Hmm...you have been neglecting your feet," he chided me. "This should have been tended to some time ago. It will pain a bit when I cut the nail. Make sure that you don't expose it to any source of infection. I will put a medicine but you keep it covered till it heals."

Skilfully, he got to work, using his sharp scalpel, tweezers, special scissors, and nail clip. Sessions with Mr Dutt have a charm of their own. Not just watching his dexterity but also listening to his nuggets of wisdom. "Many ask me the secret to my youth," he said, when I commented on how fit and fresh he looked. With a mischievous glint he added, "There is an energy point on the hand, which if pressed every day, brings a glow to the face. That is a secret I will share with you. But, more importantly, I am disciplined, eat a minimal amount, and I love my work. That is the mantra to my cheerfulness.

All day I travel by public transport but when I sit down to work, the tiredness goes away. The saying 'work is worship' is entirely true for me."

Somehow, the conversation veered into the realm of god and spirituality. "I have a simple take on that," he said. "People have altars and puja rooms for their gods, but I have my lap. I carry the altar with me wherever I go. I don't need any of the embellishments normally associated with an altar or a puja room like *diyas*, candles, flowers, incense sticks, offerings of food, and the like. My god needs me to be clean and in a happy state of mind to serve him, because then his throne is also comfortable and helps him relax."

Intrigued, I looked at him questioningly.

"Yes, I do. Does that surprise you? I am very protective and possessive about my lap and choose carefully who has access to it. My wife, children, and grandchildren have a right to it and no one else. No one, other than my god."

Even more perplexed I asked, "And who is that god?"

"Oh. The one that gives me my bread and butter, of course. The one, because of which I can live a life with dignity. The foot. It has helped me nurture my family, my dreams, and my sense of self."

"So, you carry your altar and the service is conducted in various destinations, wherever your god calls you from. It is a special relationship that you have with your god!"

"It is a unique bond that I have. I can see my god in every foot that I care for. My god has given me my purpose in life and continues to be the driving force behind my waking up every morning, going out into the heat and dust, rain and thunder, cold and fog. My god helps me contribute and makes me feel worthwhile.

There is more. My god gives me access into the homes of people from all walks of life. I remember an incident when the security stopped me from entering the residence of the governor. They looked dismissive when I told them what my profession was. I simply stated that I would happily go away but my presence in that regal mansion was because the governor needed my services, and not vice versa. I asked them to inform the governor that I was leaving because they were not allowing me in. They did not expect this response from me and on checking with the gentleman, apologised to me, and cordially escorted me inside!

Senior police officials, professors, school teachers, corporate heads, businessmen, housewives, have all been my clients. I have never felt that I am any less than any of them because when their troubled feet are on my lap and in my care, they need me and I feel needed. It helps me too. It is an interesting life and so you understand why the foot is my god. I have my own living god, whom I can serve."

And here I was, struggling with my journey for spiritual upliftment. Meditation, chanting, listening to motivational discourses, trying to cleanse energy points, reading biographies of sages and saints, seeking the perfect guru for guidance (and being a miserable disciple who questioned everything and was never convinced with the answers), visiting sacred sites in the hope of a glimmer of enlightenment, trying to get lost in trance-like music, and ultimately running a marathon without having moved a millimetre. The harder I tried the more disappointed I felt. My search for god had been like a trudge through the desert sand, getting momentarily bewitched by a mirage, and the reality crushing my faith and belief.

And here was this man, who simply did what he loved doing, did it sincerely, listened to his heart, and found his private route to his creator without any fuss.

This astounding philosophy stunned me into silence. It put me in a meditative mood as I gazed at my feet with an all new respect. No longer did it merely exist at the periphery, but was as important as my head and heart. For someone it was even the embodiment of the divine! And, what was more was that it had a warm, cosy lap as its altar when required!

15

Wee-Wee Experiences

Just before boarding a flight or a bus, in between long rides while stopping for a comfort break, the importance of the wee-wee excursion cannot be over emphasised. I've had my fair share of these stops, when the tour director breaks us out of our slumber with, "Okay, ladies and gentlemen, wakey wakey, time for a breakey...and the 'inmates' of the huge bus tumble out, heading for you-know-what, trying to outrun the others to be the first in the queue.

It was during one such excursion, as I shut the door of the cubicle, and was just about to get down to business, when I felt something tickle my ankle. Abandoning all calls of nature, I sharply turned and found my ankle imprisoned in the clasp of a human hand, travelling from under the panel that separated the cubicles. If you imagine the pre-fabricated cubicles, you will visualise the scene, since the dividing panels are a few inches above the ground, permitting easy access.

Gulping a scream, I took a deep breath and listened. It was a desperate plea. The problem was multiplied, because I did not understand the language, but such dire distress calls are beyond the confines of tongues. It was an emergency request for toilet paper, which I was fortunately able to fulfil, under the dividing board, securing freedom for my ankles.

Neither of us saw each other and would not have recognised the other even if we did. But in my restful moments, my mind sometimes wanders to the incident, and I wonder if I'll be able to recognise those hands if I chance to see them again, with Mona Lisa nail work, a sun tattoo on the wrist, and black and white diamonds sparkling on the long fingers.

I move on to a rather unusual experience.

As usual, it was a long queue. The women's loos are notorious for this and a test for mental patience and physical control. The serpentine lines always frighten me, especially if the tour director has set a deadline of fifteen minutes for the comfort break. Get back in time, or else.

You make four-minute friends during those shared waits in frustration, and they often lighten the pressure, again both mental and physical. One such line had two women standing in front of me, both carrying covered musical instruments. I asked politely, to distract myself, "Are you musicians, playing for a band?"

"Oh yes," came the reply in unison. "We're going for a concert and we don't let go of our instruments for a second. So, here we are carrying them into the restroom."

I smiled in acknowledgement and at their enthusiasm. And then, before I could comprehend what was happening, they turned around and walked smartly into the men's side—no queue—and disappeared for a few minutes.

There were just a few surprised eyebrows and confused looks as the men entering were unsure whether they were in the correct place. The duo then walked out, returned to the female zone, touched up their makeup, brushed their hair, and breezed out. It was almost like a fashion trend that went viral for a short while.

The queue disintegrated as other daring women furtively looked left and right and took over the men's side. They strolled out without a care in the world, leaving a bunch of confused and helpless men not knowing which side to turn to, forming a serpentine queue of their own.

Another incident comes to mind.

Women's restrooms in public places are interesting zones. A lot goes on there. But this particular incident was just bizarre. I read about it in the newspapers, and since then have kept my antennae alert for a repeat performance.

A newly married couple was returning from their honeymoon. At the airport, the wife deposited her cell phone and a packet of food with her husband, and toddled off to the washroom with her handbag. The husband waited dutifully for her return.

The minutes ticked into nearly an hour and he got anxious. He then took the help of the staff. They checked all the bathrooms but no one of her description could be found. Announcements were made but she did not show up. Finally, a missing person's diary was lodged, and footage from the close circuit camera was replayed. His wife had gone into the bathroom clad in jeans and a top and never exited and out had come a burqa-clad lady who had never gone in. She walked out of the exit gate into the arms of a man waiting outside!

I recall one other experience.

As usual we had the clock ticking for us to make our way back to the tourist coach. And, as usual there was a winding queue that had wound itself out of the confines of the restroom. There was in reality no rest in the restroom. If anything, it was a restive and edgy bunch of women waiting their turn, for the magic door of the cubicle to open, and one less person to wait for. This particular wait was also accompanied by a lot of chatter, revolving around the facility provided in the cubicle. All of them were in the squatting style, which of course most were unfamiliar with and unused to. It required a level of fitness and dexterity that many did not have.

Inside one toilet, was a senior citizen with knee arthritis. She carried a cane for support. Bereft of her cane, she had to balance herself on the two slabs. This was an impossible task for her. Fear of slipping into the hole made her cry out loudly for all outside to hear. Precious minutes were whizzing, pressure was mounting, tempers were failing, and patience was at dangerously low levels.

Then an angel stepped into the act. Also a senior lady, she called out to the woman in distress. "I can understand your predicament. I have had a knee surgery so I know the pain. Let me guide you. Is that all right with you?"

A while later came a weak, "Yes. I am so scared of losing balance."

"Don't panic. Take a couple of deep breaths. Now, understand that you do not have to do any gymnastics." She continued to speak to her calmly and the matter was managed. It became like a team goal, of helping the lady through the obstacle challenge. Women waited with baited breath, and then the cubicle door opened with a stressed but beaming lady-with-a-cane stepping out. There was a spontaneous, 'hurrah' and immediately someone else rushed into the vacant cubicle. There was one less person in the line.

There is another wee-wee event I remember.

It happened during the interval in a movie show. There were several films running in the multiplex, and the toilets were too few in number to cater to the large crowd. I remember we were watching a thriller and the interval had been placed at a particularly tense moment. It was imperative to be back in time for the second half, so as not to miss a 'tilting' point.

It was a single file of impatient women and the first person in the line, entered whichever cubicle fell vacant. Things were going smoothly until one woman entered the restroom. She stood in front of the mirror, brushed her already fluffed-up hair, and as soon as the door of a cubicle next to her opened, walked in before the person in the queue could.

In a flash, there were two other women who rushed and entered the cubicle with her. "How dare you break the line? Have you no basic manners? We have all been waiting and who do you think you are, barging in?"

Voices were raised, angry words were exchanged, and the truant woman was forced to step out and go right back and stand in the line, to wait for her rightful turn. Meanwhile, the first person in the queue, a mild, gentle lady was requested to go in. The message, "Don't meddle with those anxiously waiting to discover the identity of the killer in a murder mystery!"

Here is the next story in this series.

Travelling to new places has its own challenges—weather, food, language, transport, etc. But for me, a special challenge is mastering the bathroom fittings. On entering a hotel room, I usually take time off to understand the intricacies of the shower, the hot and cold water outlets, temperature management, and the like. Public toilets, too, have their own demands. Soap dispensers come in unique styles, where you can push, pull, press, lift, and what-have-you. I wish they would standardise the stuff.

The other day, on one such 'outing', I met a lady in the autumn of her life, wearing what was once a nice, black coat, close to tears. On enquiring what had happened, she pointed at what appeared to be an alien faucet or a tap. On coming out of the bathroom, she had gone to the basin to wash her hands. It was all the new stuff, with sensitised exits for water and soap. So, she put her hands near one such eye and was met with a spurt of foam, white frothy stuff that covered her hands. She rubbed it and was met with a squirt of water. She was just getting used to this when a third device got activated, a built-in blower in the system. Now, the bubbles were still on her hands and the blower was a sudden shock that sprayed the bubbles onto her black coat. The poor woman was traumatised. She asked, weakly, "Is there any normal, old-fashioned tap that I could use?"

Following is a scary wee-wee experience.

This brings me to a discussion some of us were having after dinner on the scariest experiences of our lives. A few friends had got together, and we were sharing true incidents that had elements of horror to them. The most common ones had the touch of the macabre or the supernatural. Mira was listening quietly, and then came forward with hers.

In her forties now, she was all of seventeen when it happened. Not having found a friend who could join her, she had ventured out on her own to watch a play. One of those things teenagers do as a rebellious act. Her parents did not approve of her going out alone in the evenings, but she was determined to try out her fledgling wings.

Towards the end of the play, Mira needed to go to the toilet which was at a distance from the hall. Unlike the busy moments, when it was teeming with people, it was unsettlingly quiet. The door had a lock, where you had to press a button.

Mira turned the handle when she wanted to get out. Nothing happened. Maybe she had got it wrong. She turned it to the right and then to the left. It would not budge. Her palms felt clammy, her heart beat faster, and her mouth felt dry.

"Help," she shouted, banging on the door.

No luck. There was no one around to respond to her call as she beat against the solid slab of wood. This incident was way before the cell-phone era, and there was no way to reach out. Worse still, her parents did not know where she was. As soon as the play got over and the people streamed out, the central lights were switched off. Mira spent the night in the dark public toilet, scared out of her wits. It was only the next morning that the janitor found her, collapsed in an exhausted heap.

"And guess what the name of the play was?" asked Mira.

"What?" was the response, as all pairs of eyes and ears turned towards her.

"*Behind Closed Doors,*" she replied.

And now for the final episode of the wee-wee experiences.

By the time we reached the forest guesthouse in a remote part of North Bengal, it was late evening and the group was tired with stiff backs and sore backsides from the bumpy drive. Everyone craved a comfortable bed and hot soup. The building was one of those old, wooden structures with a large verandah in front. The kitchen was a fair walk from the main building, as were the toilets. It was single-storied with large rooms and high ceilings. The toilets had two doors. One was the entrance from the building, and the other opened into the backyard, which was used by the staff for cleaning.

It was very close to the jungle. As expected, the electric voltage was abysmally low, and at times we could just about see the glowing filament. We were advised to carry a torch at all times after dusk. I felt quite lost unpacking in one corner of the huge room, then stretching out on the bed on the other side.

It was around 1 am when I needed to visit the loo. The large bowl of soup, three cups of tea, and water were taking their effect on the system. And so, I gingerly stepped out of bed, groped around for the torch, and made my trek to the toilet.

For an urban, apartment-bred person, the sheer walk was quite challenging, and by the time I reached my destination the pressure was on. While making myself comfortable in the semi-darkness, my eyes caught a pair of glistening circles at one corner of the bathroom on the opposite end to where I was. It was close to the back exit, which I now realised was only partially closed. With trembling fingers, I focused the torch on the object.

It was a bear! It is hard to gauge the reactions of the two parties. I was practically frozen with fear until necessity made me breathe again. I was curious to know what the bear was experiencing.

Obviously, this was its safe haven at night, and here I was, encroaching. The poor creature had probably sauntered in through the backdoor in search of some respite from the cold outside.

Steeling whatever active nerves were left in me, I stood and slithered towards the door, switching off the light. After what seemed like a century, I found the latch, unbolted it, and scooted as fast as my wobbly legs could carry me. Half-running, stumbling, dragging myself, I reached the dozing old *chowkidar*[1] who was sitting all wrapped up in a blanket. Huffing and puffing, I somehow managed to convey to him what I had just seen. He listened patiently, his passive face registering no emotion.

This bothered me all the more. When I had finally finished blurting out my verbal diarrhoea, he answered most casually, "Oh, were you not informed? We advise our guests not to use that bathroom at night. Bhaloo comes in there on most nights for his nap, and we don't like to disturb him. He is unused to being troubled by anyone, and your presence must have shocked him. Now that you know, ask your friends not to use that toilet for the rest of your stay here."

Honestly, I did not know whether to be angry or amused by his sheer disregard for my feelings, and his complete sympathy with Bhaloo. Either way, I learnt to respect the unwritten code of the guesthouse!

---

[1] Guard.

16

Aam Kheer

The sunlight gleamed bronze and gold, forming a diffused halo behind my daughter as she sat on a mat on the floor in all her finery. The warm glow of the sun caught the tendrils of her hair that had escaped the scented flower garland around the loose bun at the nape of her neck. I looked at her happy face as her aunts and cousins fed her spoonfuls of some of her favourite food. This was the Bengali custom of *Aai buro bhaat* or the last meal that she was having at her parents' as an unmarried daughter of the house. The wedding ceremony was the next day. Memories of her as an infant, then as a little girl growing into womanhood, flooded my mind and spilled out of my eyes. I was finding it hard to hold back my tears. My little Mishti had lost her mother years ago, and I had tried to fill the vacuum the very best that I could.

The silver plate, glass, and bowls, had been arranged in front of her, as was customary for this function. Each had some item she loved eating. What was the idea behind this ritual? I wondered. Let her leave her *baper bari*[1] with happy memories for a source of strength in her

---

[1] Parental home.

new home, to fulfil all her desires in case her cravings could not be expressed or satisfied in the new alien environment. Or, was this just a way her near and dear ones could express their affection, feeding her something she enjoyed? Whatever the answer, it was heart-rending for me to see, as it seemed like the last bugle playing before the sun set in my home.

Joyous teasing and peals of laughter floated into the nooks and crannies of the drawing room that opened into the balcony. I wished I could capture the full-throated guffaws, the gentle admonishings, the small arguments, the intense debates, the soul of our bonding, not just in the crevices of my mind but as live, tangible, holdable things. "Mishti, don't fill yourself with just *ghee bhaat*[2] and *deem-aloo sheddo*[3]," my sister told my daughter. "I've cooked your favourite prawn curry with coconut milk and mutton with green chillies, *gondhoraj lebu*[4], and *dhone pata*[5]. Leave some space for that."

"Oh, *Pishi*[6], I wish I had two stomachs. One for all this and the other for all the desserts," Mishti answered, revelling in the affection and attention.

And then came Rontur Ma[7], our very old house help who had been with Mishti all her twenty-three years.

---

[2] Ghee (clarified butter) and rice.

[3] Boiled potatoes and eggs mashed together.

[4] Aromatic lemon.

[5] Cilantro/coriander leaves.

[6] Paternal aunt.

[7] Rontu's mother.

"Mishti Ma, ami aam kheer baniyechi tomar jonno. Nishchoi khabe.[8]*"*

Mishti's face lit up. *Aam kheer* had been her absolute soul and comfort food ever since her toddlerhood. I could see her waddling up to the centre table in the drawing room with a determined, focused look of utter concentration, gripping the bowl of *aam kheer*, lifting it to her mouth, and devouring it.

To rewind time was one of those impossible and unattainable longings. I can only replay the memories over and over again. And imagine. And cling on to time and helplessly watch it slipping away.

I remember my wife giving me serious advice with twinkling eyes, "Plan differently for your daughter's future. Instead of investing in gold ornaments like most Indian parents, gift her fruit orchards, especially mango. Her husband will have a tough time meeting her appetite for fruit!" We both laughed loudly and spontaneously, visualising the scene, and our little Mishti toddled up to us, enjoying the cheer.

Temperatures were rising as with any summer day and all the activity and excitement were tiring me out. I had hoped for a winter wedding, but the groom could get adequate leave only in summer. So, here we were, in the midst of the heat, arranging a mega event in Bankura, West Bengal.

Mishti had managed to manoeuvre through all the vegetarian and non-vegetarian dishes and had finally

---

[8] I've cooked mango kheer (mango pudding) for you. You must have it.

reached the *aam kheer*. I had been clicking for posterity and had set the camera for the moment when she would partake of this favourite item of hers. I had named her Mishti, after her love for mango *kheer*. Mishti took the spoon and I adjusted the lens.

I looked through the eye of the camera. My very being froze. Standing behind Mishti, on the balcony, was a figure with a faintly mocking smile. My limbs were immobile but my mind raced. Just before Mishti put the spoon to her lips I shouted, "Mishti, stop!"

It was over twenty years ago. A memory I did not wish to replay. If only life gave the option of the erase button. Or time generously allowed a chance to rewrite an event. And give it a different ending. It only happened in dreams. Absurd ones, where one was befooled into believing that everything had been set right.

I was in charge of a jail that is known as a correctional home now. The date was December 12th. It was in the early hours of the morning that I stood before a young man with intelligent, piercing eyes. There was a calmness about him that I could recall clearly. He had been condemned to die by hanging, for a political murder he had committed, under the misguided zeal of youthful passion. The deceased had been responsible for taking many innocent lives, and had struck terror in the region. He had also killed the young man's elder brother.

The brother was a dynamic young leader, who had exposed the corruption of the murdered man and others involved. The man was the kingpin of an underworld operation that ran multiple businesses in drugs, illegal arms, and black marketeering in various products. He was protected by his connections. The brother had managed to collect enough evidence against him and made it public. He paid with his life.

On the day of the hanging many had assembled in front of the jail, because their sympathy was with the young man. But law has to take its course. At one level, I felt sad for the lad, and disturbed at having to oversee the hanging. The boy seemed to have a lot of promise. Given the opportunity and the right guidance, I believed he would do good work.

He, on the other hand, had accepted his fate. I could not help but ask, "Why did you have to kill him? Look at where it got you. If everyone starts killing each other, where will it end?"

"I have no fear of death. I believe I have delivered justice. My job is done. Not only have I avenged my brother's death, I have also done a cleansing act for society at large, and am prepared to face the consequences. It was not something we started. But a bullet has to be matched by another. Instilling fear cannot be one man's prerogative. And living in fear is for the cowardly. It is not an option for me. The game had gone on for too long." It was the fire of young blood speaking, ready to take on the world, his way.

I had a duty and a job to perform, whether I liked it or not.

As per the custom, I asked him if he had any last wish that he wanted fulfilled. He thought for a moment, smiled and said, "Yes, sir, I do, but I don't think you can fulfil it. So, it is better for you not to know it."

Intrigued, I insisted that he tell me.

"Sir, I have always enjoyed chilled *aam kheer*. My mother made it for my birthday each year. I would request you to fulfil this as my last wish before you put the noose around my neck—just a bowl of chilled *aam kheer*."

On hearing this, my throat felt dry and I mumbled, "Okay, let me see." I knew this was not a wish I could fulfil in the middle of winter. This was not the mango season. Today, with all the benefits of technology, there are options of procuring unseasonal fruits and vegetables, for a price, since they are imported. Not so then. I did make enquiries, hoping against hope, for some magical intervention. No unseen hand intervened.

Time cannot be rewound or rewritten.

And so, the young man had walked into the chamber with a hint of a mocking smile, saying, "Sir, I told you not to ask me about my last wish. I knew you would not be able to grant it."

Over two decades had passed and somewhere I had pushed the troubled memory deep into my subconscious. I had failed a man his last desire. Today, he was back and standing there—with the same slightly arrogant, mocking smile, claiming the fulfilment of his last wish. The universe was granting me an opportunity to make amends and I needed to grab it with both hands. We had unfinished business, and I had to make peace with his spirit.

"What happened, Baba?" Mishti asked, quite bewildered at my behaviour. She added jokingly, "Don't tell me I have to wait till you finish adjusting your camera lens."

For a moment I was at a loss about how to respond. No one else seemed to see the figure standing firm behind Mishti. What could I tell them? I had to think of something. With slow, deliberate steps I went to my daughter and sat beside her.

Speaking softly, I said, "Mishti, in all the excitement I forgot to do something important. We need to offer one item to our *kul devata*[9] before you complete your meal. This is an auspicious occasion. Since you have not yet tasted the *kheer*, let us offer this bowl. There is more. Rontur Ma will get you another bowl, and I want to feed you the *kheer* myself."

Mishti looked at me with a warm smile and hugged me closely. "I am so happy you will feed me my most favoured dish, Baba. Some of my fondest memories are of you feeding me dinner and telling me a story when I was too sleepy to eat it myself."

While embracing my daughter, my eyes strayed to the image standing behind her. "Finally, I could fulfil your wish. Please enjoy the *kheer*." My eyes urged him, and he looked at me and smiled, a benign, happy smile. This time there was no hint of arrogance or mockery.

---

[9] Family deity.

It was a genuine, contented smile of a young boy saying "thank you".

For me it was a release, a relief from the guilt I had been carrying deep within me.

17

Why Not For Me, Ma?

Parvati had woken up before the sun. Bathed and cleaned, hair washed and oiled, she was ready to welcome the *Surya devata*[1]. "This is a ritual as old as mankind itself," her mother had told her. "You need sons, as strong and sturdy as the *Surya devata* and your fortunes will shine like the sunbeams. He is multi-faceted, strong, giver of energy, and good health."

Parvati had absorbed the information in sincerity and unquestioning faith. After all, her mother had done it, and so had her mother before her. They had had sparkling lives with husbands and sons cocooning them. So what if Parvati herself had been born a girl, and had looked after her parents just as much if not more than her brother? Someone had to be born a female, and get all the blessings to womb a male child.

She had done all that was expected of a *good girl,* not entered the puja room or the kitchen on '*those*' few days. She'd kept a fast without drinking even a sip of water to beget an ideal husband, continued the fast after marriage for the well-being of her husband, and now starved herself for the welfare of her two sons, the sunbeams in her life. The daughter was, after all, only a

[1] Sun god.

guest. She would be married off to another family and household, hopefully to perpetuate their family name, by giving birth to a son. Her boys were her investment for her future comfort.

Parvati was twenty when she got married. She lived in a joint family with her parents-in-law and her father-in-law's elder brother's family. Eager to 'fit-in' as she had been trained, she tried to do what she could, to please the seniors. What was not in her control was the gender of her first born.

"Oh! It's a girl. Hopefully, your next child will be a boy. We need to have a torch for our family name. That is your greatest responsibility, Parvati. To keep the family name going strong," were the cold, dismissive words of her aunt-in-law, also a woman! Parvati could sense the disappointment all around. The tension of living in the unforgiving environment was unbearable. So pervading was the sense of blame that after a point, Parvati started feeling guilty about having let down the family.

Her husband, on the other hand, welcomed the baby girl and named her Laxmi, the goddess of good fortune. Unfortunately for Parvati, he was then posted in another city and visited only occasionally. She had no respite from the hostile treatment of the family.

Two years later when the twin boys were born, it was almost like a rebirth for Parvati. There was celebration in the family and for the first time, she felt accepted as a family member. It was her boys who appeared to be her gateway to freedom from oppression. Never once did she think of questioning the system that was perpetuating the ill treatment. She was happy and relieved and grateful to her boys. Her mother's words echoed inside her, her sons would make her fortunes shine!

It was a weekday, and her three children were getting ready for school. She took the *prasad*[2] for her twin ten-year-old sons, and as they grumbled about the milk and swallowed the fruit, she put some of the *prasad* in their mouths. It was a special puja that she did annually, only for her sons.

"So, what are you cooking for us today? After all, it is our special day, dedicated to the sons," they laughed and teased their mother. Their favourite items had been packed for their snack, and lunch would be equally appetising. The centre of a lot of fuss and importance in the family, they had grown up accepting their dominance as most natural. "I have sports today, and Ma, why are my shoes not polished?" asked one of them, spouting irritation.

"Oh, I am sorry. Just give me two minutes and I will have it ready," apologised Parvati, as she hurried to get the whitener.

In all this flurry of activity, Laxmi was quietly getting herself ready for school. The eldest of the three children, she was twelve, and knew she had to do her own work herself. She had been broken into the system early in life, but unlike her mother, had questioned it. Parvati had tried convincing her that her salvation lay in keeping the gods appeased all the time, even if she did not believe in it.

---

[2] Food that had been served to the deity.

"You will suffer for this," she had warned Laxmi when she refused to follow in her footsteps, as she had followed meekly in her mother's. Laxmi was more confident than her mother, had a mind of her own, and often argued with her mother.

"But I get irritated only when I am forced to do something I don't like. I will not touch the feet of all the seniors who visit us. Some of them have filthy feet and that uncle who visited us yesterday, I hate the way he touches me. I will do *pranam* only to those people I like."

"You are a girl. Behave like one. How many times will you fight? You just have to accept that it is easier to keep quiet and do your duty or what is expected of you. This world is a cruel place for girls who do not conform."

"How do you know that? You have never even tried to question anything. I have seen you crying when your sons speak rudely to you, but you still continue to do all their work. Why don't you speak up? I cannot be you and neither do I want to be."

Today, suddenly, Laxmi was feeling even more frustrated with the unfairness of the system. Thoughts raced through her mind. "Am I not important? Do I not count as one of the children? How can Ma be so partisan? What about some special food, *prasad,* and prayers for me?"

Smart enough to realise that her mother would be dead to her queries, she sat silently, watching the play, as it were, being enacted. Her father, too, was an early riser, not to appease the gods, but for his own interest. He would go for an early morning walk and have a cup of Darjeeling tea on the balcony, as he read the newspaper and waited for the morning tornado to blow over. The family was in emergency mode, getting ready for the early morning school bus. He knew better than to question his wife's religious and ritualistic beliefs and practices. Previous attempts had drawn a complete blank. He had his reservations regarding them.

That morning, he observed Laxmi. She looked unhappy as she watched her mother and her brothers in action. He understood his daughter well, and could sense her feelings. Casually, he walked up to her and, putting his hand around her shoulders, popped a special sweet into her mouth.

"This is for you. You know I don't do any special puja but I decided to keep a fast for my daughter today. Ma is doing it for your brothers, and I want to do it for you. It will help me lose some weight too, don't you agree?" He hugged her and smiled.

Laxmi gazed up at her father, her eyes glistening. She, too, was important. She, too, was valued. Life was not so unfair, after all!

A voracious reader, he would share stories with Laxmi, whose favourite pastime was story-time with her father. "Not that I want you to become like the character I am going to tell you about, but it has an important message," he told her one evening, his eyes twinkling. Her brothers were busy with their karate teacher.

"This happened over a hundred years ago. There was a band of dacoits who carried out some very daring attacks. As you can imagine, the dacoit *sardar*[3] had to

---

[3] Leader.

be a man with exceptional strength of personality, to be able to lead the band. He had a son and a daughter, who were one-year apart in age. He had been trained by his father to develop leadership skills. He was also training his son and daughter, though it was unusual for a girl to be trained. He was the fourth generation in his family, who had been the *sardar*. They all led from the front and needed a lot of courage, charisma to motivate the group, and excellent fighting skills.

During one of their raids, he was mortally wounded. The question arose about who would become the next chief. What do you think happened?" asked her father.

"It was a gang of dacoits and the father had trained his son, hadn't he?" came Laxmi's spontaneous reply.

"Yes, that would appear to be the most expected course of action, given their profession. But the reality was different. The band *chose* the daughter as their leader, over the son. In *her* they found all the requirements of a leader. They felt they could respect her and she would guide them and lead them as was needed."

Laxmi's eyes were shining with excitement. "So, what the story says is that if you have the qualities in you, you will be recognised, regardless of your gender. In what seemed like an all-male job, the daughter could take the challenge."

Though brought up in a male centric, conservative environment, Laxmi's father had broken out of the mould early in life. He had observed his father deify his mother and yet coerce his own wife into subservience. The apparent dichotomy confused the boy and he had decided never to replicate it. He had spent his college years in a hostel, read widely, and developed his own world view. He realised that his wife was being subjected to similar treatment like his mother had been, and at the earliest opportunity managed to get a posting out of the city so that he could set up an independent unit, free of the stranglehold of regressive thought patterns.

He could succeed in giving his daughter breathing space and the freedom to grow with an independent mind. Often she and he would listen to the song 'Born Free', which they both enjoyed very much. He could not, however, alter his wife's mindset, though she enjoyed all the freedom.

And so, the three children grew up, the boys with a sense of entitlement and Laxmi with the knowledge that she was loved and valued for *who* she was, not merely because she happened to exist. She qualified as an architect and was living in a high-rise apartment in a gated-community. Married to a fellow architect, she had moved to Mumbai from Kolkata. She was expecting a baby after three months. Her brothers, also married, were posted in Bangalore and were software engineers, managing their own start up.

A sudden heart attack took their father away. Laxmi's mother was ailing too and could not manage to live independently. The decision of where she would now stay loomed large. There was a family conference on the matter. The brothers claimed lack of space in their flats to give her a separate room on a permanent basis. She was welcome to visit occasionally. The problem remained.

Laxmi knew her mother had reservations about living in her daughter's house. "How can I live with my daughter? That is your husband's house. I have sons, with whom I have a much stronger right to stay," she argued.

"But under the circumstances that option is not there," Laxmi tried to convince her, as gently as she could. "My husband is very happy about you living with us, and you can always visit your sons. His mother too lives with us and you both can share a room. The good thing is, you both like each other. See the brighter side. You will have company."

And so her mother moved in to live with Laxmi. The due date came closer and Laxmi took off from work. One evening, when mother and daughter were talking over a cup of tea, her mother held Laxmi's hands and said, "I sincerely pray to my *Surya devata* that you have a daughter, just like you."

About the Author

Sumita Banerjea is an author and educator. An alumna of the Convent of Jesus and Mary, and St. Stephen's College, New Delhi, she has done her PhD in History on "Crime Against Women And By Women In Bengal In The 18th And 19th Centuries". She has written school textbooks on Geography and English and has also written for various newspapers and magazines. During her time as an educator, she conceptualised and edited an anthology of writings by school children in the senior classes. She is also trained in psychological counselling and conducts workshops for corporates, teachers, and students.

Sumita loves to experience life in a myriad different ways: travelling, teaching, writing, counselling, listening to happenings in the lives of people from various walks of life, and telling stories. She lives in Kolkata.